TALLOW

An Urban Legend

MJ Howson

Engine ❶❸

THE **TALLOW** SERIES

Copyright © 2018 MJ Howson

Second Edition.

First published in November 2017 under ISBN 978-0-9996166-1-1.

Published by Engine Thirteen

ISBN: 978-0-9996166-3-5

Cover design by MJ Howson

for Dad

Prologue

Urban legends are born from truth. To ignore them is to become their prey. Their history and story may change over time. But only the foolish would believe they could never happen again.

Urban Legends of Cape Cod

Author – Unknown

ONE

Sara

Sara Johnson frowned as she inspected the busted rear door of the gift shop. It was a chilly afternoon in Truro, Massachusetts. Temperatures were hovering around 40 degrees. She looked down at the variety of wood screws spread out next to her knees and shook her head in confusion. The strike plate had been completely ripped from the doorframe. Large chunks of wood were scattered across the stock room. The cold November air blew across the open door and past her face. Sara had tried a variety of different sized screws, but the wood frame was completely torn apart. There was simply no way to reattach the strike plate so that the door would stay locked. Slowly, she frowned in disgust. She had hoped she would be able to easily repair it herself, but the damage from the break-in the other week was beyond her skills.

"I don't really have the time for this," Sara said.

She groaned as she pulled herself upright. Her right thigh throbbed in protest as she stood up. She put the screwdriver she had been fumbling with back into her small bag of tools. The wind suddenly blew the door wide open. Shards of wood rushed past her winter boots. Sara put her gloves back on and slammed the door shut. She then slid the tool bag up against the door to keep it closed.

"That should hold it," Sara said.

The broken door would have to wait. Her priority today was getting the place ready for the new inventory that would be coming in tomorrow. Sara turned and exited the stock room. She glanced around the dimly lit store, looking for the perfect spot to showcase the new merchandise. Power was out, but it was a sunny, if windy, afternoon on the Outer Cape. There was enough time to get things set up before darkness set in.

Sara stood alone, quietly inspecting the layout of the store. The space was quite crowded, with a variety of stands and displays spread across the floor and against the walls. As with most gift shops on the Cape, they sold just about anything you could think of.

"This place is a mess," Sara said with a sigh. "I'm just going to have to jam some stuff together to make room for the new display."

Sara walked toward the center of the store. There was a small square aluminum table with four piles of T-shirts stacked on the top. A sign in the middle read, "Buy One Get One Free!" She held one of the shirts up and looked at the front of it. The shirt was light blue and had an image of Cape Cod in bright white across the chest. Below the image, it said "Truro" in vivid red letters. She rolled her eyes as she dropped it back onto the table. *Tourists.*

"This space will do best," Sara said.

An oversized wooden table sat off to the side of the one with the Truro T-shirts. She tossed the shirts onto the larger table. Sara grabbed the sign with one hand and the lightweight table with the other and carried them back into the stock room. Her gait was slow, and she moved with a bit of a limp.

In a dark corner, behind the rear entryway, sat a round wooden table. Sara had unloaded the table from her Jeep prior to attempting to fix the door. The table had been handmade by her father. She thought the unique design would add a touch of hominess to the store, as well as be an eye-catcher.

Sara picked the small heavy table up and carried it out to the spot she had cleared in the middle of the store. Her right leg throbbed lightly as she struggled to carry the table. She gently set it down and took a few steps back to inspect the placement. She made several adjustments to get it perfectly centered in the open area.

"There," Sara said. A small smile of self-approval spread across her face. "If you are watching from above, Dad, I hope you are proud."

Suddenly, her phone rang. The chime coming from her jacket pocket startled her.

"Hello?" Sara asked as she answered the phone. After a brief pause, she nodded. "Yes, everything is all set. I just got the table in place. But I couldn't fix the back door. I might need your help with that."

Sara bent down and noticed how dirty the legs of the table were. She took a glove from her pocket and began to dust the nickel and turquoise inlaid legs, hoping to bring a nice shine back to them. She continued to nod as she listened to the voice on the other end of the call.

"Bad news?" Sara asked. She gripped her leg as she stood up. Her eyes widened at what she heard next. "Anna is dead?"

Sara shook her head in despair. She fought to stop the tears that were welling inside of her. The voice on the other end of the phone continued explaining what had happened, but Sara was no longer listening. All she could think about was the loss of her friend. She wiped her eyes and did her best to regain her composure.

"OK, I understand," Sara said. "I'll be OK. Anna was just very special to me. You know that."

Sara walked to the front of the store and glanced out at the fading light. There was no power to light the store. She knew she had to finish up before it got too dark. Her mourning over Anna's death would have to wait.

"OK, thank you for telling me," Sara continued. "I have a bit of cleaning to do before I leave. I will be home soon."

Sara ended the call and placed the phone back into her jacket pocket. The weekend would be here in a few days. Most of the businesses had closed up for the season, leaving her with little competition for attracting tourists. A storm was in the forecast for the weekend. She knew it would limit her customer flow, but she was determined to remain optimistic.

The news of the loss of her friend now motivated her to move forward. She turned her back from the giant windows along the front of the store and headed toward the door that said "Employees Only."

The stock room had a small bathroom in it with various cleaning supplies. Sara went through her options and grabbed a bucket, a few old rags, and some bleach. She filled the bucket with hot water and then returned to the front of the store. Off to the side was the checkout counter. She walked behind it and glanced down at her next project.

So much blood.

The cabinet below the cash register was splattered in blood. Dark crimson streaks ran down the sliding aluminum doors. The tracks were filled with blood. A dried puddle of blood had formed a small circle on the old, warped wooden floor.

Sara's eyelids fluttered as her mind briefly recalled the horrible attack that had occurred the other day. Her palms became sweaty, and her heart began to pound hard in her chest. Images of a blood-soaked dagger ran through her mind. Suddenly, she pictured Anna being butchered. She clenched her right thigh and felt her knee begin to buckle.

"No!" Sara cried out.

Sara opened her eyes and took a few deep breaths as she caressed her wounded leg. *You survived. You survived!*

Sara looked at the carnage sprayed out before her. She knew she had saved the worst for last. This final task was something that could not be avoided. The bloodstains had to be cleaned up before the store could be opened. She felt her pulse begin to return to normal. A sense of calm washed over her.

Sara assessed the situation. The stains across the back of the cabinet would be easy to clean. The old wood floor, however, would be more of a challenge. The varnish had worn away from years of shoes scuffing across the floor behind the cash register. The exposed natural-toned wood was now splashed with a deep maroon color, mimicking a cherry wood stain.

"Maybe I should just stain this entire area," Sara said with uncertainty. "Or perhaps just use a throw rug to cover it up for now."

Sara began to slowly and methodically wipe down the back doors of the cabinet. The blood stains were less than a week old. They had dried to solid streaks, smeared across the plastic fake wood laminate. With a bit of pressure, the gore from the prior weekend's horrific events quickly disappeared.

"If my mother could see me now," Sara said solemnly. "What was it she said? 'In times like these, we all have to make sacrifices.' Indeed, we do."

TWO

Tom & Julie

It was a typical early December day in Providence. Although it was almost noon, the sky was gray, and the temperature had peaked at a crisp 40 degrees. Sun would not be in the forecast for the weekend.

Tom was sitting by the window in his kitchen, reviewing a printed copy of his Travel Checklist. A hot cup of Earl Grey tea sat to the left of his list, a pencil to the right. Tom always made a checklist when he traveled, no matter the length of the trip.

For this particular trip, there were some last-minute surprises. The most concerning was the weather. That gray, dreary sky outside his kitchen window was the beginning of a storm front slowly rolling into the New England area. Tom and two friends were heading east today to spend the weekend on Cape Cod. The trip had been in the works for weeks. Weather forecasts in New England were often a roll of the dice. Tom was twenty-eight years old and had spent his entire life in Rhode Island. He knew all too well that even the worst doom-and-gloom forecast could often turn out to be nothing major.

Tom glanced up to look at the small television mounted to the wall of his kitchen. He had the volume muted. The noon weather forecast was starting with a special announcement. An official Blizzard Watch was in effect for the southern half of the state.

"Great," Tom said with a sigh.

He glanced down at his list. Hat, gloves, and scarf were already there under the "Clothing" section, marked as packed. He took a sip of his tea and smiled. It was such a thorough list. He had sections for all the things that had to be done, divided by when they needed to be done. Each item on the spreadsheet even had a formatted box he could easily check off as he went along.

Tom scanned down to the end of the list where he had several blank lines for last-minute items. He grabbed his pencil and wrote, "heavy-duty boots."

Suddenly, the deadbolt on his front door snapped open. Tom did not bother to glance over. He continued to scan through his spreadsheet, looking for items he may have missed.

After several seconds and some banging, the door flew open and bounced off the back doorstop. His friend Julie Perez stood in the doorway, draped in baggage. She grunted as she shoved a big rolling duffle bag into the hallway.

"Hey, Jewels," Tom called out.

"Max! Max! Max!" Julie yelled. "Aunty Jewels is here!"

"He's not here," Tom replied. "I already brought him to my Mom's."

"Damn!" Julie said.

Julie kicked her bag further into the room, dropping her purse and a second bag on the floor. Tom frowned and stared at the hardwood floors. *Does she not know that hardwood floors can scratch?* The word "polished" was never one he would use to describe Julie, or "Jewels," as he called her.

"So, when did you drop Max off?" Julie asked. She began tugging at her purple leather gloves with her teeth, trying to get them off.

"After his morning walk and breakfast, around 9 a.m."

Tom had adopted Max, a German Shepherd mix, from a no-kill shelter two years prior. He stood just above knee-height and weighed fifty-five pounds. Max looked like a German

Shepherd puppy but was fully grown. Luckily for Tom, his mom was semi-retired and was more than happy to watch Max anytime Tom had to travel. During the weekdays, when Tom was at work, Julie would stop in to let Max out at lunchtime. Her office was only a few blocks from Tom's condo.

Julie tossed her coat and gloves onto a chair in the living room and walked into the kitchen. She sat at the table, facing Tom. He looked down at her boots. Julie frowned.

"I kept my boots on because I thought we would be leaving soon," Julie said. "Besides, they are a bitch to get off."

"It's fine," Tom said. His response was not very convincing.

Julie pulled her knit hat off and dropped it on the kitchen table. She purposely let it cover Tom's spreadsheet.

Tom sighed and pulled his spreadsheet back so he could see all of it. Julie smiled.

"How's your anal little list coming, Tom?"

"On track."

"Should I assume you have 'Bring Max to Mom' on there and it is all checked off?"

"What do you think?"

They both laughed.

"So, you must be all packed and ready to go?"

Tom pointed to a small carry-on bag next to the front door, along with a knapsack that was leaning against it.

"That's all you need?" Julie asked.

"Jewels, it's only two nights. You look like you have a week's worth of clothes."

"What can I say? I like options. I see you have your little geek pack. What do you have hidden in there for this trip? The usual suspects?"

Tom always brought his knapsack everywhere he traveled. If he were flying it would be his "one personal item," and he would tuck it under the seat. It had everything he would need in case of emergency as well as all of his electronics. This would include items such as his laptop, tablet, headphones, audio connectors, and power cords. Along with his geek toys, he would also pack things like food, tissues, and napkins. His Travel Checklist had a section just for items to put in the knapsack.

"Well, for this trip I'm not bringing my work laptop or my personal laptop. So, I only plan to have my tablet and charge cords. But I also have this new thing I bought just for this trip. It's a portable power source. Think of it like an external battery. You plug it into the wall to charge it, and then you can use it on the fly later to run anything with a USB jack. I figured it would come in handy."

"You are just amazing," Julie said with admiration.

She and Tom had taken countless vacations together. Julie could ask him for the most random thing, and he would pull it from that knapsack -- gum, candy, dental floss. You name it, and chances are he had it in that bag. She figured one day she would surprise him and request a tampon as the ultimate test. But she feared he would actually have one ready for her.

"Did you hear from Marc yet?" Julie asked.

"Nothing yet."

"I wonder if he and Chris patched things up yet."

"I hope not. She gets on my nerves. It's always drama with those two. This trip was just supposed to be the three of us."

"You've never really warmed up to her."

"I just don't see her and Marc together long-term. Do you?"

"I don't know," Julie answered. She sighed as she looked out the window at the gray sky.

"It's been almost a week since they had that big fight," Julie continued. "My money says that Chris caves and comes along. Marc is way too hunky for her to say no to. I couldn't resist those big brown eyes of his. Could you?"

"Do I smell a secret crush, Jewels?"

"Oh my God! No!" Julie said, laughing. "Please. The minute I met Marc I could tell he wasn't interested in me. I don't chase. No matter how pretty they are. And he is a very pretty man. They make such a striking couple."

"You think so?"

"On the outside they do. But it has definitely been a bumpy year of dating for them."

"Dating is overrated."

"Says the guy that hasn't been on a date in the past year."

"I'm on sabbatical."

"Oh, please," Julie said with a chuckle. "You just ..."

Tom glanced up from his cup of tea and waited for Julie to finish her sentence. She paused.

"OK, Tom, you enjoy your sabbatical."

Julie leaned over the table and used air quotes to emphasize 'sabbatical.'

"We can discuss it another time," Julie continued. "Besides, we have more important things to talk about. How's my hair?"

Tom chuckled. Julie was a master at defusing any potential powder keg of a situation. He didn't know anyone who could change topics as fast as she could. Julie was also correct to question her hair. That knit hat had created a static mess in her wavy brown hair.

"Well, I don't know what your mom would call it," Tom replied. "What's Latin for 'train wreck'?"

Julie jumped up from the chair and ran to the bathroom to check out her hair.

"Oh my God!" Julie shrieked. "You know my ya-ya actually knitted that hat for me. She sent it over from Greece for my birthday. My dad was so thrilled. I thought the style was both retro and tragic at the same time. It was ... retragic! Now I know it's also massively static-inducing."

Tom grabbed her hat from the kitchen table and looked it over. It had about seven or eight different colors in it, woven into a pattern of blocks and stripes. On top, it had a giant purple pom-pom. He would never have guessed her grandmother had made it for her. It looked store-bought.

"Do you have a hairbrush anywhere?" Julie asked.

"There should be one in the drawer in the bathroom vanity."

Julie tried the drawer on the left. Sure enough, there it was. Julie pulled it out and inspected it, taking note of the short blond hairs tangled in its bristles.

"Are you losing your hair?" Julie teased.

"No!" Tom yelled.

Julie laughed as she started to brush out her static- ridden hair.

"We should go to Greece someday to visit her. Or maybe go see my abuelita in Colombia. The men in both those countries would go crazy for a little white boy like you!"

Tom laughed.

"Let's plan that for next year, Jewels."

"Hey, what's the latest on the weather forecast?" Julie asked. "I really haven't been paying attention. I thought I heard snow or something."

"We're in a Blizzard Watch."

"Really? Shit. So, wait. What's worse, a Watch or a Warning?"

"A Watch means we need to keep an eye on it. A Warning means it's definitely going to hit. Well, as definite as the weather forecasters can be."

"It's a good thing Marc's truck has all-wheel drive. We should be fine."

"I still wish we were taking Ruby. I just had new reservoir shocks installed on her yesterday."

"Ruby" was the name Tom had given his Jeep Wrangler. He had bought it at the beginning of the summer. The local dealer had a fantastic price on a one-year-old demo they were looking to unload. It was a two-door Sport model in Firecracker Red. He'd wanted a Rubicon model, but it was too far outside of his budget. Tom planned to spend the next year customizing it. His mother let him store Ruby's doors in her garage anytime he wanted to remove them. He and Julie had enjoyed numerous runs to the beach with the Jeep earlier this summer.

Julie emerged from the bathroom. Her dark brown hair was back to its usual long wavy style.

"I for one am super excited about this weekend," Julie said as she sat down at the kitchen table opposite Tom. "Road trip! I love road trips! And I'm dying to see Marc's new condo. I'm sure it's fabulous. He's a contractor, so you know it will be amazing. I mean, look at the job he did on your kitchen."

Tom looked around his kitchen. He had to agree with Julie. His kitchen had turned out beautifully. The space was small, roughly eight feet by twelve feet. Tom had hired Marc in September of last year to renovate the kitchen. The condo had been a bank-owned sale, and the prior owner had not done any upgrades. All of the rooms were serviceable, but nothing close to what Tom had envisioned. Someone at the gym had recommended Marc. Tom thought he knew how he wanted the new kitchen to look, but Marc helped take it to a whole other level with a lot of custom woodwork and lighting elements that made it a step up from the ubiquitous white cabinets and stainless-steel appliances.

Tom's phone chimed.

"Speak of the devil!" Tom said. "It's Marc."

Tom looked at the text message and frowned.

"What?" Julie asked.

He held up the phone so Julie could read the message.

Hey Tommy. FYI Chris is joining us.
Waiting for her to arrive. ETA 30 minutes
or so.

"I knew it!" Julie said. She was thrilled to hear that Chris was joining them. The look on Tom's face, however, told her he was far from happy.

"Relax, Tom! It'll be fun! Adventure awaits! Vacation weekend! This will be the first time the four of us go away together, won't it?"

"Exactly," Tom sighed. "Up until now, it's been nothing more than day trips. I can barely tolerate her for a few hours."

"I seriously don't know why you two fight all of the time. So much bickering. It's bad enough that Chris and Marc have their own monthly blowouts. You need to relax and just have fun. Enjoy the vacation. Look at it as an opportunity to get to know her better."

"If you say so, Jewels."

Tom leaned back in his chair and let out a deep sigh. "Thirty minutes until the fun starts."

"Thirty minutes. my ass!" Julie retorted. "Chris will be late. And Marc runs later than Chris! Those two do not understand the concept of punctuality. I say at least an hour."

"Ditto on that, Jewels."

"So, did he tell you any more about the townhouse he bought?"

"Marc told me the place is mostly furnished, but the renovations are only half-done," Tom answered. "He sort of had a bit of a power struggle with the developer. Marc wanted to buy the place with the kitchen and bathrooms totally empty but the developer wouldn't agree to that. So, they compromised a bit.

"Marc's been running out there the past few months to oversee the installation of all the custom components he asked for. He even brought a bunch of stuff out for them to install. But he said he plans to do a number of additional upgrades over the winter."

"Well, 'half-done' to Marc means it is probably still awesome to us."

Tom took a gulp from his mug, finishing up the last of his tea.

"Oh," Tom said. "While we're out there, I need to pick up a Christmas gift for my mom."

Julie's excitement over the upcoming trip suddenly took a nosedive.

"And what is her royal highness requesting this year?" Julie asked. "A custom tapestry made from 100% Egyptian cotton hand-sewn by children rescued from Martha Stewart sweatshops?"

Tom frowned.

"She's not that bad," Tom said. He paused, then smiled coyly and added, "The kids don't have to be from sweatshops."

Julie laughed.

"All she wants is a candle," Tom said.

"Oh, please! I seriously doubt it is *just* a candle. I can already tell you are going to be dragging my ass into every gift shop on the Outer Cape. Spill it."

Julie was not a fan of Tom's mother. She took every opportunity to keep Tom away from his mother's sphere of influence. Julie was actually the one who convinced Tom to buy this bank-owned condo. His mom had objected because of the risk involved. Julie was thrilled when Tom sided with her. To this day, however, whenever there's an issue at the condo, his mom will weigh in with, "Well I told you not to buy it." It drove Julie crazy.

"Last week I painted her bathroom for her," Tom said. "Three of the walls are blue, and one is light tan. Doing two different colors was my idea, but she picked out the colors. She is doing this whole beach theme. All she asked for was a blue or tan candle to match the new colors."

"And?"

"A nice scent."

"And?"

"Well, more specifically a nice beach scent."

"And?"

"Something about the design that makes it special. Nothing off the shelf like you would find at any sort of big box store."

"And?"

"And what? That's it!" Tom said with his voice raised. The line of questioning really began to annoy him.

"OK, so a blue or tan beach-scented candle. Local thing. Got it. Actually, that's really not that bad for her. Is that on your spreadsheet?" Julie said with a laugh.

"No, silly. That's my travel list."

"Oh right. Don't you have a list for shopping?"

"Actually, I have an app that I use. And yes, the candle is there. God, I really am anal, huh?"

Now Tom was laughing. Julie let out a slight snort as she laughed louder.

"Oh my God, don't make me snort! Well, if you want my advice, which I know you don't, I would get her something completely different. She keeps you under her thumb. Surprise her! Get one of those LED candles."

"Surprise her?" Tom asked. "Jewels, you've met my mother. She does not like surprises. Besides, if I don't get her exactly what she wants, I'll just get the guilt trip for the next decade. I can hear her now. 'Sorry, the bathroom is not the complete beach design it should be because I don't have a properly scented candle in there.' Trust me, it's much less painful to get her what she wants than deal with the aftermath."

"She really does lay the guilt on you, Tom. Are you sure your family's not Jewish?"

"Trust me ... I'm starting to wonder myself. There must be some buried in my French Canadian and German DNA. You know I was raised a good Catholic boy."

"No comment. But seriously, I don't know how you put up with her. She's annoyed me since the day I first met her. Has she always been this bad?"

"I don't know. All I can tell you is everything went downhill after my dad died."

"Oh ... right. Sorry. I didn't mean to bring up ..."

"What about you?" Tom asked, quickly changing the subject. "Is there anything special you want to buy while we're out on the Cape? Christmas is only a few weeks away, you know. Maybe some static-free yarn for your ya-ya?"

"No, I don't have anything special to buy," Julie replied.

Julie got up from the kitchen table and walked over to the living room to the pile of bags she'd left on the floor. She picked up her purse and started to rummage through it.

"You know me," Julie said. "I just love to window-shop. Besides, it's December. Half of Cape Cod is closed this time of year. There may not be many shops open. So, my expectations are low on the shopping front. I do all my gift shopping the weekend before Christmas anyway."

Julie continued to hunt through her purse. She stopped and stared at the wall and tried to think. *Where is it?* Julie dropped the purse and grabbed the other small bag that was next to the large duffle bag. She began to search through it.

"I brought something for the car ride and nights around the fire," Julie said. "Wait, does this place have a fireplace?"

Finally, she found what she was looking for. Julie dropped the bag back onto the floor, where it landed with a thud.

"I'm not sure," Tom said. "It would be nice if it did. If not, Marc will just build one."

She came back into the living room carrying a small paperback book. It was roughly five inches by seven inches and maybe a half-inch thick. It looked new. She sat down at the kitchen table with Tom.

"What is it?" Tom asked. "A book on how to lose a man after three dates?"

"Oh, please. Don't you even go down that road!" Julie said, laughing. "Besides, when were *your* last three dates? Two years ago?"

Tom clenched his fists under the table. He set himself up

for that one. He didn't want to start a discussion with her about dating. He loved Julie to death, but once she got on her soapbox, it would often turn into a very long lecture.

"One point to you, Jewels. Now, what about the book?"

"It's a book about urban legends of Cape Cod."

"Urban legends?"

"Yes! All those creepy stories of ghosts and disappearances and things that go bump in the night. Unsolved mysteries. Missing persons. Witches."

"I know what urban legends are, Jewels. But you hate scary movies."

"I know!" Julie said, chuckling. "My dad gave it to me for my birthday a few weeks ago. Said I needed to get over my fears. He was joking, of course. Stumbled across it in a gift shop when they were on the Cape this past summer. I figured it would be fun to flip through during the drive out there. Possibly even lighten the mood if necessary."

"You mean in case Chris and I get in a spat."

"Or Chris and Marc. Hey, it's better to be safe than sorry. Can you make me some hot cocoa?"

Tom picked up his empty mug and headed over to the counter along the back wall of the kitchen to fill his electric teakettle. He filled a large measuring cup with filtered water from the fridge and poured it into the kettle, flipping the power switch to "On."

"I only have instant. I hope that's OK."

"Damn, you make the best hot cocoa from scratch. That's fine, though. As long as it has those fake marshmallows?"

"Of course, Jewels."

"You're the best!"

Tom grabbed another Earl Grey teabag for himself as well as a package of instant cocoa mix - with marshmallows - for Julie. He leaned against the kitchen island as he waited for the water to boil.

"What's your prediction on those two?" Tom asked.

"What do you mean?"

"Marc and Chris. As a couple. They seem to break up every month or two. It's been almost a year now since they first met. Do you see this going the distance?"

"I don't know, Tom. But I'm the wrong person to be asking. I mean, I go through men like tampons."

"I won't argue with that, Jewels," Tom said with a chuckle. "But seriously, do you see it leading anywhere?"

Julie paused to gather her thoughts. Her and Tom's opposing viewpoints on love and dating often resulted in heated arguments.

"I have my doubts," Julie finally said. "Don't get me wrong. I love them both. First of all, you have two supermodels side by side. I mean, Marc is your textbook tall, dark, and handsome. Smoking-hot body. Super sweet. Calm and laid back. He owns his own business, so he's also successful and obviously has some serious cash. That condo he bought had to cost him a fortune. Chris is just as sexy. I love Chris! Nobody makes me laugh like she does. I mean when we get going ..."

"I know, Jewels," Tom interrupted. "I swear you two feed off each other laughing like little schoolgirls."

"Chris totally gets me to start snorting!"

Tom shook his head in agreement.

"But they are just massively opposite. That can be a good thing if the differences complement each other. In their case, I think the differences clash. Opposites never last."

"Gee, Jewels, if I didn't know any better, I would think you're speaking from experience."

"You know I am, Tom! Don't get me started on that idiot David that I dated this past summer. Oh. My. God. Talk about opposites. I'm willing to compromise to some degree, but when it's constantly all about the other person you need to just walk away. That's where you and I differ. I can spot when things aren't going to work early on so I cut that cord. You can't. Or maybe you do and choose not to ignore the impending doom."

Tom frowned. They were supposed to be talking about Marc and Chris.

"Jewels, the reason you can so easily cut the cord is because of your fear of commitment."

"Oh, please!"

"Hey, if you want to start comparing dating trends then let's put all of our cards on the table. I know I can get clingy and fall fast. When was the last time you actually fell in love with someone? Sure, you date more than I do. But have you ever fallen for any of them? What's it been, like five or six years since you had a serious relationship?"

"Hey, at least I've had a long-term relationship!"

Julie instantly wished she could take back her words. She knew Tom would give anything to be in a committed relationship. Things just never seemed to work out for him.

"Sorry, Tom," she said in a quieter tone. "I didn't mean to snap at you like that. Let's table our dysfunctional relationships and focus on the one going on between Marc and Chris."

Tom looked over at Julie and she flashed him a big smile. He smiled back.

"I like that idea," Tom agreed. "I get your point about Marc and Chris being opposites. Chris is also a bit of a party girl. She lives for weekend pub crawls."

"Seriously! And that is totally not Marc. Like I said, deep down they are opposites. That's why they have these blowouts every month or so. Those differences keep bubbling up."

"They do break up all of the time," Tom said. "Too much drama for me. Relationships should not be that volatile."

Tom glanced at the electric kettle. He could hear the water inside starting to boil. He looked back over at Julie.

"I also think Marc shouldn't be dating someone eight years younger than he is."

"And there it is!" Julie said, letting out a chuckle. "I knew that was coming. You're just jealous because you're not the baby in the group anymore."

The beep on the electric teakettle signaled the water was ready. Tom turned around and grabbed a new mug for Julie's cocoa. He poured the water into both mugs and added the cocoa mix to her mug, turning back to face her.

"That's not it," Tom continued. "Chris is twenty-five, and Marc is thirty-three. She is too immature for him. I also think Chris is using Marc for his connections in the real estate world."

"Seriously? I don't see that at all. I agree about the age difference, but she doesn't seem like a user to me. She can be a bit of a drama queen, though. You sound like you are coming up with a ton of reasons not to like Chris. The two of you are always getting in fights. It has been that way since they started dating. If I didn't know any better, I would think you're jealous."

Julie laughed as she pointed both hands at Tom in a taunting way.

"Oh, please," Tom said as he rolled his eyes.

Tom turned his back toward Julie. He reached into one of the drawers in the kitchen and removed a spoon. He gently stirred the mug of cocoa and did not turn back. He kept his focus on the mug and waited for her to continue.

Julie paused as she stared at the back of Tom's body. She had made that comment as a bit of a joke. Now she wondered if maybe she had struck a nerve.

"Marc likes to fix things," Julie continued. "He's a contractor. Maybe he sees Chris as something that can be fixed? Personally, I think Marc is just a hopeless romantic. To answer your original question, I just don't see this going the distance."

Tom let out a slight smile. He was glad to hear that he and Julie were on the same page.

"I say we just let that relationship run its course and see how it plays out," Julie added. "It's really not our business anyway."

"Not our business? We just ripped them both to shreds behind their backs!"

Julie started to laugh and snort. Tom grabbed the two mugs and brought them around the island and over to the table next to the window. Julie raised her cup of cocoa and inhaled deeply. *Nothing beats hot cocoa on a cold winter day*, she thought to herself.

"Their ears must be burning," Julie said. "We can be so evil! I swear we're going to burn in hell. Hey, did you happen to pack some snacks in your geek pack? Marc is so damn healthy. You know his pantry will be boring as shit."

"Like you have to ask, Jewels. You know I always take care of you."

"You're the best!" Julie said, smiling at Tom. "Hot cocoa

mix, too?"

"Why do you keep asking questions you already know the answer to? Trust me. You will be pleasantly surprised with what I have packed for you."

"Yay!"

Julie took a sip of hot cocoa and stared out at the cloudy gray sky.

"I really hope this is a fantastic weekend," Julie said. "Promise me you'll make an effort with Chris. Even if we both think their relationship is doomed, let's have a fun time. This should be all about Marc and his new condo. Holiday shopping on the Cape! Road trip!"

"I'll do my best, Jewels."

"I promise to do my best to play referee and keep things fun."

"I know you will."

Tom turned his attention back to the television mounted on the wall. The meteorologist was still talking about the blizzard. Tom grabbed the remote and turned the TV off.

"We should really kick this road trip off with some champagne," Tom said. "But I don't have any chilled. So why don't we just pretend? We can be classy with our mugs."

"You know I am all about being classy!"

They both laughed.

Tom held up his cup of tea. Julie raised her mug of cocoa.

"May I propose a toast, Miss Perez?"

"Why of course, Mister Leblanc."

"Here's to a fun-filled, blizzard-free, shopping-filled, drama-free weekend."

Tom and Julie clanked their mugs together.

"Drama-free? With those two?" Julie asked. "We should be so lucky."

"Ditto on that, Jewels."

THREE

Marc & Chris

The huge plastic tub that Marc Sirloa was carrying was testing both his balance and strength. He was now second-guessing his decision to pack all his cast-iron pans into a single bin. The thin plastic bin definitely wasn't meant for a load this heavy. But he only had about another twenty feet to go to reach the back of his truck. Marc quickened his pace as he could feel the edge of the handles digging deeper into his fingers. Gloves probably would have been a good idea as well. Luckily, he was able to reach the truck and slide the tub in without dropping anything or slicing his hands open.

"I think that should do it," Marc said aloud, as he glanced around his empty driveway.

Marc had underestimated the volume of what he wanted to take to the Cape this weekend, but he was pleased that he'd managed to fit everything into the truck. He had closed on his new investment property in early September, but that was prior to the completion of construction.

Over the past three months, Marc had made a half-dozen trips to the Cape. The two-hour drive, in addition to running his own business, prevented him from being as hands-on as he would have preferred. He spent many of those visits working on the place. He had negotiated a number of custom items into the design of the unit. At first, the developer of the new complex had resisted. But, as they worked on the components of the deal, the developer eventually came around. In fact, the developer liked some of the design elements so much that he was planning to replicate them in the other units that were under construction.

The bulk of the construction on Marc's place was already completed. He had told everyone the condo was still a work in progress, but the truth was it was in move-in condition. On his last trip out to the Cape, he'd had the furniture delivered for the unit's two bedrooms, the living room, and the dining room. Even Chris had no idea how much of it was done.

This trip was all about filling up the cupboards and closets. He had a mix of new and old items to bring -- dishes, pots and pans, glasses, sheets, towels. He knew there was a lot he was missing, but he planned to do an inventory with Chris after everything was set up and then see what they could find in town. He also hoped to find some great artwork by local artists.

Aside from putting the finishing touches on his new place, the trip was a chance for everyone to get away and have some fun, especially him and Chris. Their fights seemed to be escalating in both frequency and intensity over the past few months. Marc had yet to identify a common trigger or event or topic that would set Chris off. Their arguments always ended the same way, with Chris giving him the silent treatment for a few days until he could convince her to give things another try. The last blowout, however, had been the worst one yet.

Marc knew they needed time alone to talk, but he also knew that having Julie and Tom come along would keep things fun. Chris loved spending time with Julie. To say that Chris and Tom were struggling in their friendship would be an understatement. Marc was counting on Julie to be the entertainer, and perhaps even help Chris and Tom become better friends.

"What am I missing?" Marc said as he looked over his truck bed.

He had removed all of the packed containers from inside the house. Chris had helped him box it all up last night. Everything that was going to the new condo was packed tightly into the back of his pickup truck. He also had a few empty bins ready for any luggage items that people might want to secure. Marc had placed tarps across everything in the bed. The waterproof canvases were ready to be locked down tight for the long trip ahead.

Marc looked at his watch. They were running very late. *Where is she?*

As Marc studied the contents of the pickup bed, a black BMW X3 came zipping around the corner.

Chris Becker was running late and knew it. She turned into Marc's driveway and pulled next to his truck. The BMW jolted hard as Chris abruptly slammed the transmission into Park and popped her door open.

"Hi," Chris said as she stepped out from her SUV.

Marc smiled at the sight of her, as he always did. It brought him back to the first time he met her. For Marc, it had been love at first sight. It was hard for him to believe they'd been together for an entire year.

Marc met Chris at a high intensity interval training class at the gym. Marc was mesmerized watching her go through the kettlebell swings. Her long blond ponytail bounced up and down across her back as she displayed near perfect technique. She was fit, but not overly muscled. She was soft and feminine and curvy. To Marc, her physique was perfect. Marc knew he had to talk to her. He rushed through his shower and then waited by the exit to start a conversation with her. When she finally emerged from the locker room, Marc knew he was smitten. He complimented her on her form during the class and asked if he could walk her to her car. The two started dating the following weekend.

"Babe, did you want to pull the car up toward the top of the driveway?" Marc asked.

"No. If that blizzard hits, I don't want you to have to dig my car out. If I park right at the end I can just easily pull out when we get back."

"Smart thinking."

Chris walked to the back of her SUV and popped the hatch. She pulled out two matching Gucci carry-on bags. She glanced over at Marc's huge pickup truck.

"Do you have any empty bins to protect my bags?" Chris asked.

"Of course."

Marc walked over to help Chris with her bags and paused as he stood next to her. At five-foot-ten, Chris was about four inches shorter than Marc. He glanced down at her porcelain face and smiled.

"Hi, gorgeous," Marc said, waiting for a warm reply.

"Hey."

Chris leaned in and gave Marc a quick peck on the cheek. Marc pulled her close and gave her a long embrace.

"I'm glad you came by last night," he said. "It was a good talk, wasn't it?"

Chris stayed silent as she let her head rest against Marc's chest. Marc kissed the top of her head.

"I wish you would open up," Marc continued. "These endless fights, Chris. I just don't get them."

Chris tilted her head up, but said nothing. Marc looked deep into her green eyes. Normally bright and dazzling, they seemed dull and lifeless today. The gray skies reflected off of Chris' tortoise-rimmed Gucci glasses, dampening the mood even more. Chris forced a smile and looked away quickly. Marc sighed, realizing she had her walls up.

"I'm glad you're here," Marc said. "You were a big help last night."

"Well, I did promise you I would help with setting up the new condo. I keep my promises."

Chris let go of Marc and turned back to her vehicle.

"Let me help you with the bags, Babe."

"I have it. You can just get the bins."

Marc walked over to the back of his truck and pulled out two mid-sized plastic tubs from the pile he had stacked inside. Chris dropped a carry-on into each one. The lids were separated and packed on the left side of the truck. Chris took two lids and secured the bins. She locked the handles in place and put the containers back into the truck.

"I hope you packed your workout clothes so we can hit the gym this weekend," Marc said.

"Of course."

Fitness was one of many things they had in common. Marc was fairly strict with his diet regimen, avoiding almost all grains and sugars. He had spent the summer trying to get Chris to follow the same diet. She did her best. However, on the weekends Chris would put that diet on hold to enjoy some much-deserved alcohol. She had a feeling booze would be a large part of this weekend trip.

"Do you think we should take two vehicles?" Chris asked. "I could follow in mine. Then you won't have all of this stuff exposed in the back of your truck. Julie could ride with me."

"You sound like Tommy wanting to take his Jeep."

Chris winced. She hated it when Marc compared her to Tom. She also hated that Marc called him "Tommy." It sounded too affectionate. She ignored the comment.

"Well, with the bad weather forecast, shouldn't we have a vehicle that we can protect stuff in? My BMW is all-wheel drive so I won't have trouble keeping up with you if the weather gets nasty."

"It's just a little snow. Nothing to worry about."

"A little snow? It's going to turn into a blizzard! I mentioned that last night when we were piling everything up in your hallway. It was on the news."

"Babe, those weather forecasts are always wrong. We never get a ton of snow this early in the season. It's not even officially winter for a few more weeks. Relax. I have tie-downs and tarps to cover everything. Ninety percent of this will be left at the new condo. The bed is just going to be piles of empty containers for the ride home. Besides I want us all together for the drive out. It will be fun!"

"If you say so."

"It will also give you and Tommy some quality time together. You two butt heads way too often. Why do you always turn into such a brat with him?"

Chris stuck her tongue at Marc.

"C'mon, Babe," Marc said, trying to stifle a laugh. "Why?"

Chris didn't respond.

"Christine?"

Chris glared at Marc. She did not like being called by her full name.

"Well, he is just way too much of a control freak. Thinks he knows everything. He doesn't! Someone needs to put him in his place. You and Julie just coddle him. I'm the only one that calls him out on his bullshit."

Marc laughed.

"I just wish you would make more of an effort with him." Marc continued. "I know he can be a pain in the ass sometimes. Why not treat him like you do a client? You're really good at your job. You work hard to win your customers over. Even the ones that drive you crazy. You always compromise when you have to at work. But you make everything a competition with Tommy. Everything. Why? Look at how fantastic you and Julie get along."

Chris smiled.

"Julie is the bomb!" she said. "I love that girl. If you want me to have a fun weekend, let her and I ride together in my car. We'll laugh our asses off nonstop."

"Well, the reason things work with you and Julie is because you both laugh everything off. Everything is silly. A joke. With Tommy, you make everything into a contest."

"I make it a competition? *Me*? You always take his side, Marc. Even last weekend when we had that game night. He had to gloat over every win and rub it in my face."

"Babe, it was just a game. Nothing more. Julie also beat you a few times but you just laughed with her. There is a total double standard going on in how you treat those two. You can do better."

Chris paused. *Why do I have to be the one to take the high road?* She wondered.

"OK, Marcus," Chris said. Marc shook his head. He knew Chris well enough to know that "OK, Marcus" meant "OK, Marcus, I am over this and moving on."

Chris took a few steps back and looked up at the dreary sky. She paused and took a long deep breath. She needed to shake off this discussion. She walked around to the side of the massive pickup. She looked at the writing on its side: – Sirola

Construction, Providence RI. The silver Ram 1500 was only a year old, but it already had its share of scrapes and scratches along the fenders.

"So, is everything packed?" Chris asked. "It seems pretty full. Do you want me to rearrange all of this for you to make more room? Can we fit whatever Tom and Julie have?"

"No, it's fine, Babe. I have a system. Don't change it. Let me go do one last look inside the house."

Marc jogged back up the driveway and disappeared through the front door. He needed to let Chris defuse. He could tell the discussion about Tom had upset her.

Chris walked around the back of the truck, inspecting Marc's packing job. He had indeed managed to pile quite a bit into the bed. Peeking through the spacing between the tarps, Chris could see all the boxes of newly purchased dishes and some small appliances. There were also several cardboard boxes that she had helped Marc pack last night. There wasn't a ton of room left to add more bins. As successful as Marc was, he was not always efficient. Not to mention forgetful. Chris mentally assessed the stacked boxes and bins and quickly determined she could easily gain more space at the back of the truck with just a few adjustments.

I can improve this, she thought to herself.

No matter how much she hoped, Marc was never going to be an organized person. Well, at least not as organized as she would like him to be. Chris removed her glasses and tucked them into the case in her coat pocket. She only needed them for distance and driving. She quickly started to undo a few of the tie-down straps so that she could get a grip on the boxes and bins. They were packed in tight. Chris felt they were just in the wrong direction.

Chris looked up at the house. Marc had left the front door open. She shook her head in disappointment, thinking about all the wasted heat flying outside. *It must be nice not having to worry about paying your heating bill each month.*

Turning her gaze back toward the bins and boxes, she decided she needed to make some small changes to rearrange it all.

Chris jumped into the bed and began pulling items back

and to the side. She was able to make a sort of tunnel down the middle without fully removing the tarps that Marc had put in place. They were just loose enough to give her maneuvering room. Once she got to the back of the bed she started to swivel the boxes. She methodically went one by one, twisting any box that would better be served going across instead of front-to-back. It didn't take long for everything to loosen up. She also took the time to stack some of the boxes so the shorter ones were on top. Within a matter of minutes, Chris had managed to gain another foot of space along the back of the pickup bed.

"What are you doing, Babe?" Marc asked.

He had returned from the house and was standing next to the back of the truck. Chris was sitting on some of the empty bins in the back bed, smiling.

"I was adjusting the boxes."

"I didn't realize anything was wrong with them."

Chris frowned.

"You had a lot of them turned the wrong way," Chris explained. "It wasn't an efficient use of the space. Now I have it so that most of the handles are all on the left and right sides. It will make unloading a lot faster, plus it gave you more room."

Marc did a half smile. As was often the case, Chris was attempting to correct a problem that didn't exist. Marc had arranged the boxes and bins so that the contents could be easily identified when looking at it from the back of the truck. All of the labels faced out. He figured that would make it easier to unload and carry them to the right room. They had also been grouped together by room. But he wasn't going to point this out to Chris. He knew this was not worth arguing over.

"I got you something," Marc said. He pulled a small booklet from his coat pocket.

Chris hopped down from the pickup and grabbed the book. It had been rolled up into a tube. She unfurled it and looked at the cover with confusion. It was a real estate catalog for Cape Cod.

"What's this for?" Chris asked.

"I thought you might want to check out what the properties are like out on the Cape."

"Why?"

"For down the road."

"Marc, we've discussed this. I'm barely surviving here in Providence. Those lease payments on my BMW kill me. You know I am still living paycheck to paycheck. I want to build out my business here. I can't even think about getting licensed in Massachusetts."

"Babe, you need to think long term. We would make a great team. You find the fixer-upper properties. I buy them. We flip them."

We? Chris could feel her blood pressure rising. She glanced down at the book in her hands and realized how mangled it was becoming. She relaxed her grip.

"Marc …"

"Don't pull away like you always do. We've now got this amazing townhome out on the Cape that we could use as our base of operations."

Chris sighed as she glanced down at the real estate book.

"We have a townhome? *We?* That's yours!"

"I just meant we can spend a lot of time out there doing research. You know I've talked about expanding my business. There are tons of great properties out there ripe for renovation. Just think about it, Babe."

Chris managed a half smile. She walked over to the front of the truck, opened the door, and tossed the book onto the seat.

"Sure, Marc."

Marc walked up behind Chris and wrapped his arms around her, pulling her back against his chest. He gently kissed the top of her head.

"Hop in. I just need to get everything tightened up, and then we can head out."

Chris turned around, releasing herself from his embrace.

"So, you double-checked everything?"

"Yes, the hallway is empty of boxes. All locked up. Heat is turned down. We're good to go."

Marc walked to the back of the truck and started to reposition the tarps and pull the straps down to lock everything back in place. Chris followed him and scanned through the contents of the bed.

"Marc, I thought last night you said something about bringing your patio set."

"Shit, you're right. It's just the little one out back."

"I can get it for you."

Chris ran up the long driveway and around to the back of the house. Marc had a small wrought-iron table they had bought together this past summer on a day trip to Westerly. It was only about three feet in diameter. Black iron. The top was a series of inlaid mosaic tiles that formed a series of red and blue flowers. The table came with two matching iron chairs. All three pieces folded up easily.

Chris smiled briefly as she recalled the many summer nights that she and Marc had spent in the backyard enjoying a bottle of wine by the fire pit. She looked around the yard to see if there was anything else that should be packed.

"Marc!" Chris yelled from the top of the driveway.

Marc had just finished securing all but the last two straps on the back of the truck. He glanced up the driveway at Chris, standing next to the garage.

"Did you want to bring the fire pit, too?" Chris asked.

"No, Babe. It's too rusted out. We'll get a new one."

We. Chris sighed.

Chris quickly folded up the two chairs and secured one under each arm. She eyed the table and wondered if she could carry that as well and do it all in one trip. An old green metal citronella candle sat on top of the table. It had a metal cover and a small wire handle for carrying, but the handle had snapped off on one end. Knowing how sentimental Marc was, she figured he would want the candle as well. She decided to make two trips and quickly walked down the driveway to the truck.

"Thanks, Babe," Marc said. "Want me to get the rest?"

"No, I've got it. You should really go double-check the house. I can finish packing it all."

"But I already looked, and ..."

"Just double-check, please. You always forget something. Go look in all the rooms."

Marc frowned but did as instructed. As he headed up to the house, Chris went to the backyard and folded up the table so that it was flat. She smiled at the efficiency of the design. It was a three-foot wide table with four stable legs that folded up to be roughly two inches thick. Chris took it and the old candle back down to the pickup truck. Marc was still in the house.

Chris loosened two straps and then moved two of the bins apart and slid the table upright and shoved it all the way to the back. Friction made sure it was securely locked in place. Marc had tucked the two chairs off to the side and they looked well-stored. She looked around for a place to put the old candle. Her bins with the Gucci bags were closest and had room inside. But there was no way she was putting that old candle in with them. Instead, she managed to wedge it between the chairs and a box marked "Kitchen." She then tightened the straps back down into place. Chris turned as she heard the thud of the house door being closed.

"All set?" she asked.

Marc approached, waving his cell phone.

"Would you believe this was on the kitchen counter plugged in and charging?" Marc asked.

Chris laughed as she jumped out of the bed and slammed it closed.

"I swear I would be lost without you," Marc said. "Let's go have some fun."

Chris popped open the truck's passenger door and dusted off some debris from the seat, tossing the Cape Cod real estate book onto the floor. She jumped in, closed the door, buckled up, and put her glasses back on. She briefly considered grabbing her prescription sunglasses, but the dreary sky was not going to clear anytime soon. Marc hopped in beside her, showcasing a huge grin. Chris smiled. She looked at Marc's handsome, chiseled face and could see the happiness beaming from his dark brown eyes. Even in December, Marc was completely tan.

"OK, so I'll do my best to get along with Tom on this trip," Chris said. "I may even let him win a few arguments, even when I know I am right."

"You are the best, Babe."

"But no card games this trip. No games, period. And there is no way I am sitting in the back seat with him."

"That's OK. I prefer having you up front with me."

Marc fired up the engine and put the truck into Reverse.

"Alright then," Chris said. "Let's go get Will and Grace and start this road trip to hell."

FOUR

Rookie

Officer Jeff Jones placed his cell phone on his office desk and sighed. The call from his mother had not contained the news that he had been hoping to hear. He checked the clock hanging on the wall at the far end of the Truro Police station. It was ten past noon. He was about to head out to lunch when Chief of Police Robert Grant approached his desk.

"Bob," Jeff said as he stood up.

"How's it going, Jeff?" Bob asked. "Please, sit. Sit."

Jeff returned to his chair and began to straighten the papers and folders on his desk.

"I'm doing ok. You?"

"Me?" Bob asked with a chuckle. "I'm great. Only a few more years until early retirement. You're the new kid in here this year. I wanted to see how you are doing."

"I'm doing well. I really enjoy it here. Everyone has been so great."

"I'm happy to hear that. I do my best to run a tight ship, but at the same time, I want everyone to feel welcome. Big plans for the holidays?"

"The usual, sir. Dinner with the family."

"How's your grandmother doing? Last time we talked you said she had taken a turn for the worse."

Jeff glanced down at his cell phone and frowned.

"Yes. She just ... continues to drift away. It wasn't the greatest Thanksgiving this year. It's hard watching loved ones get old. Get sick."

"Well, you know that if you need to take time for anything you just ask, OK?"

"Sure thing. Thank you."

"What's going on with your latest case?"

"The break-in at the store?"

Bob nodded as he sat down on the corner of Jeff's desk. Jeff opened up a folder that had been resting in front of his computer screen. He flipped through a few pages before replying.

"It's an odd one, sir," Jeff said. "No leads so far."

"Can I see the formal statements from the owners?"

Jeff rummaged through his folder and handed Bob a set of papers. Bob grabbed his glasses from his shirt pocket before attempting to read the report. He flipped through a few times and then handed it back to Jeff.

"That's odd," Bob said. "Nothing was stolen."

"That part confuses me a bit."

"That shouldn't confuse you."

"Sir?" Jeff asked.

Bob sighed as he observed the look of puzzlement wash across the young man's face.

"Someone broke in but took nothing. The store wasn't even ransacked. What does that tell you?"

The young officer paused as he stared up at the Chief of Police. Officer Jones was only twenty-six years old and had been with the Truro Police for less than a year. Robert Grant had been a great mentor to him. As a recent graduate of the police academy, Jeff not only respected his commander but also sought his constant approval.

"I'm thinking they were looking for something," Jeff finally replied. "Something specific. They couldn't find it, so they left."

Jeff smiled as he closed the folder on his desk. He realized Bob was not smiling back. Jeff began to nervously run his fingers over the scruff of his red beard.

Bob adjusted his backside as he attempted to find a comfortable position on the corner of the desk. His size thirty-eight-inch waisted trousers strained against his forty-two-inch waist. The leg of the desk groaned in protest.

"Possibly," Bob replied. "But did it look like they were looking for something? I would have expected the store to at least have things thrown out of place somehow. There was no indication of anything being searched. Even the display cases were fine. Can you think of anything else?"

Jeff's smile faded. He flipped his folder back open to review his notes. Bob watched with amusement as Jeff tried to find the answer.

"What if the point of the break-in was to break in?" Bob continued.

Jeff scratched the top of his head and stared at Bob.

"How so?" Jeff asked. "I'm not following."

Bob smiled as he stood up. He slid his thumbs through the sides of his belt and lowered the waist of his trousers to a more comfortable position.

"What if they broke in to test the store's security systems?"

"Sir, there aren't any."

"OK, well what if they broke in with the intent to return later?"

"Later? But they haven't."

"Maybe not yet."

Bob turned and headed back toward his office.

"Excuse me," Jeff called out.

Bob stopped and turned.

"Why would someone do that? For what reason, sir?"

"That, Officer Jones, is what you need to figure out."

FIVE

Road Trip

Marc checked his driver's side mirror to confirm the lane to his left was empty. He tapped the brakes to take the truck off cruise control. He'd set it at 63 mph. Route 6 was about to drop down from two lanes to one. The lane was clear, so he let the truck coast down to 50 mph. They were about two-thirds of the way to their destination, and so far, the trip had gone smoothly, with both external and internal traffic.

"Here comes Suicide Alley, everyone," Marc said.

Suicide Alley was the nickname of a thirteen-mile stretch of the Mid-Cape Highway portion of Route 6. It got its name due to the number of head-on collisions that had occurred on the road soon after it was built. Most of Route 6 was composed of two lanes on each side, heading both east and west, separated by a median. But between the towns of Dennis and Orleans, it dropped to a single lane in each direction.

There were no barriers to divide the lanes of travel, just two simple painted yellow lines separating traffic. For years, the road had been plagued by head-on collisions, as cars accidentally drifted into opposing traffic. At other times, impatient drivers crossed the double-yellow stripe to pass a slower vehicle, often with deadly results. Eventually, the government put up plastic posts between the lanes to reduce crashes. It worked, but the nickname stuck.

"So, I have a question," Chris said. "Actually a few."

Tom tensed up. Chris had been way too polite the entire trip. He feared something was brewing.

"Julie," Chris continued. "You aren't dating anyone right now, correct?"

"That's right," Julie answered from the back seat. She looked over at Tom. He just shrugged.

"The last one was that idiot from the summer," Chris said. "Was it David?"

"Please don't remind me," Julie answered.

"What's with the dry spell, Julie?" Marc asked. "I thought you wanted me to put a revolving door on your bedroom."

"Right?" Julie answered, chuckling. "I am seriously past due. Thanks for reminding me."

"And Tom, you are like permanently single, correct?" Chris asked. "I've never seen you on a date. Or are you secretly dating someone and we don't know about it?"

"Single by choice for now," Tom said.

"OK, so I want to know why you two don't just date."

Julie was the first to burst out laughing.

"Oh my God!" Julie said. "Are you kidding me? Why would you even think to ask that?"

"Um, you do know we both like guys?" Tom asked.

"Because you two are so inseparable!" Chris continued. "How do either of you expect to get into a serious relationship with anyone if all you two do is hang out together? You go everywhere and do everything together -- dinner, movies, vacations."

"Game nights," Tom added.

Marc winced. *Don't poke the bear, Tommy.* He turned to look at Chris to see how she would react.

"Hey, I let you win," Chris replied. "Every round."

Chris turned her head toward Marc, smiled, and stuck her tongue at him. He laughed.

"You so did not let me ..." Tom started to complain.

"I am half-serious, Julie," Chris said, cutting Tom off. "I mean, Tom probably wouldn't know what to do with a woman."

"Hey, just because I'm ..." Tom said.

"So tell me," Chris continued, interrupting Tom again. "Are you those two people that used to date but it didn't work out and you realized you were better off as friends? I don't even know how you two met. For all I know you were high school sweethearts. Or maybe you are actually brother and sister. Twins separated at birth. You are both the same size. Pint-sized. What, five feet tall?"

Julie laughed again. Chris was right. They were the same height.

"We're both five-six," Julie said. "But I'm like five-nine in heels."

"Ditto on that, Jewels," Tom said with a grin.

"Oh, and I weigh more than Tom," Julie added. She turned to look at Tom. "How you stay at 140 pounds is beyond me."

"It's your big boobs," Tom joked. "We would weigh the same if it weren't for those jugs of yours."

"Exactly! My Girls come at a price," Julie said as she ran her hands across her chest. "These babies have gotten me more than my fair share of free drinks."

Tom laughed in agreement.

"And don't tell me I never date," Julie continued. "I date plenty. I just rarely tell you losers about my men anymore. Look how all of you beat me up over what happened with David. I don't need the abuse. Tom's the celibate one."

"Wait, you don't know how those two met?" Marc asked.

"No," Chris said.

"Oh my God!" Julie said. "It's the best story! How can you not know this?"

"Because nobody tells me anything."

"That's because you work all of the time," Julie said. "I'm always trying to get you to hang out with me, but it's all work and no play with you."

"That's the life of a realtor," Chris said. "OK, Julie, tell me the story."

"No, let Tommy tell it," Marc interjected. "Tommy, you tell it best."

Tom had been reading some different weather reports on

his tablet trying to get an update on the storm. He flipped the cover closed and slid the tablet back into his knapsack. He looked over at Julie. She was so excited to be hearing this story again. It never got old.

"OK, Chris," Tom said. "I'm a freshman in college, studying in Providence at the Rhode Island School of Design. I commuted in from my mom's house in Warwick. Yes, I still lived at home. She insisted. Don't get me started on *that* story.

"Anyway, I found college to be a big change from high school ... in a good way. The classes there were so diverse. I wasn't stuck sitting next to the same idiots day after day. There was this one guy in my art history class. I thought he was crazy-sexy. I could not stop staring at him. He looked over and smiled at me all the time, but I never had the courage to start a conversation with him.

"One late spring day I was sitting outside having lunch, and he came up and started talking to me. His name was Rob. We completely hit it off. But I didn't know if he was interested in me because he liked me or, you know, *liked me* liked me."

"And this was how many years ago?" Chris asked.

"Like ten or eleven I think," Julie said.

"So anyway," Tom continued. "I agree to go to dinner with him. Dinner leads to, um, well, dessert."

"You go, Tommy!" Marc laughed.

"So, of course, the next day I am madly in love with this guy and can't wait to see him again. We text back and forth all day long. This goes on for the rest of the week. We see each other in class. Sometimes we eat lunch together. Dinners. Lots of desserts. Lots."

Everyone laughed.

"So, a couple of weeks go by, and I am bursting to tell him how much I love him and want us to be monogamous."

"For real?" Chris interjects. "After two weeks?"

"Hey, I was young!"

"I think it's sweet," Marc said.

"No, it's annoying," Julie added.

"So, one afternoon I text him and tell him that before we go to dinner I want us to go for a stroll along the river because I want to talk to him. He says he wants to talk to me too. I am beyond excited because I am convinced he wants to tell me the same thing."

"Good God, I already know where this is headed," Chris said.

"OK, so we are walking along, and before I can tell him how I feel, he tells me there is someone else. He tells me that I'm a great guy, blah, blah, blah. It's him, not me. The usual bullshit I hear when I get dumped. But I never saw it coming. So I am totally shocked. Devastated.

"So, he leaves me there. Basically crying. I gather my thoughts and decide I can't drive home yet because the last thing I need is to have my mom ask me a million questions about why I am so upset. So I find this little coffee shop and get a huge cup of decaf coffee.

"The place is full, and I manage to grab the last table off in the corner. I'm staring down into my coffee mug feeling totally sorry for myself. This big-chested girl my height – spoiler alert, it's Jewels – comes barreling in and sits down across from me and blurts out, 'Men suck. Can I sit with you?'"

"Wow, Julie, so you had those fabulous tits a decade ago?" Chris asked.

"Honey, I swear my Girls started developing right after I was born," Julie answered. "Maybe even in the womb."

Both Julie and Chris started to giggle.

"So, I feel I don't really have a choice," Tom continued. "I mean, she asks the question *after* sitting down. She doesn't even bother to introduce herself. She just starts venting about how she spent the past few weeks having some guy wine and dine her and when she finally 'gave him her flower,' as she put it, he dumped her."

"Flower?" Chris asked. "I love it!"

"Exactly!" Jewels laughed. "Men have to earn access to my flower."

"Says the one that needs the revolving door," Marc said.

"Well, I was a bit more picky back in college," Julie said, laughing.

"I tell her I am sort of in the same boat," Tom said.

"Except you gave up your flower on the first date, Tommy," Marc teased.

41

"He was hot! I couldn't say no. Anyway, I tell her that this guy that I really liked dumped me after two weeks because he had met someone else. She tells me that she got the same line. We agreed that men are evil."

"That's a cute story," Chris said. "And you both lived unhappily ever after?"

"Oh, I haven't gotten to the best part yet," Tom continued.

"So, we're sitting there venting and comparing notes and Jewels looks up and says, 'Oh my God … that asshole is here!' I turn around to face the entrance to the coffee shop and both of us at the same time yell, 'Rob!'"

"Wait, what?" Chris asked.

"We look at each other and at the same time ask, 'Is that the guy you were just talking about?' And then we both start laughing.

"Rob had heard us yell out his name. His jaw dropped. Total panic-stricken look on his face. He must have wondered how long we had known what was going on or if we were in cahoots on both dating him at the same time. The look on his face was priceless. Anyway, he quickly turned around and ran out the door."

"So you both met by chance at a coffee shop after getting dumped by the same guy?" Chris asked.

"It was so magically tragic," Julie answered. "It was … tragical!"

"Wait, so that means … you both slept with the same guy?" Chris asked.

"Exactly," Julie said. "He had both our flowers. We started calling him 'The Gardner' from that day forward."

Chris and Marc were laughing so hard they were in tears.

"It's all fate, guys," Marc said. "Seriously, it was meant to happen. And you two are such great friends now."

Tom and Julie smiled at each other. Julie offered up a high five and Tom smacked it. They both laughed.

"And you two never hooked up?" Chris asked. "Ever?"

"Oh my God! No!" Julie said. "I only like big, tall, hunky guys."

"Ditto on that, Jewels," Tom confirmed.

Marc wiped the tears of laughter from his cheeks.

"That story never gets old," Marc said. "We still have a ways to go. What now? Some music? More tales of sin?"

"No, I have something better!" Julie said with excitement. "Something fun!"

She grabbed her bag off the floor and started to rummage through it. She quickly found the book of urban legends.

"My dad gave me this book for my birthday."

Julie held the book up. Chris turned around and reached back to take the book from her. She tipped her glasses up above her eyes so that she could read it.

"*Urban Legends of Cape Cod*?" Chris asked as she read the title aloud.

"Exactly!" Julie answered.

"And this is your idea of fun?" Marc asked with a chuckle.

Chris inspected the front and back and then flipped through the first few pages.

"Why is there no author listed?" Chris asked.

"There has to be," Julie said.

Chris inspected the book a second time.

"I don't see one anywhere," Chris said. "Weird."

Chris flipped through a few more pages and stopped at the prologue. She spent several seconds studying it and then read it out loud:

> Urban legends are born from truth. To ignore them is to become their prey. Their history and story may change over time. But only the foolish would believe they could never happen again.

"What story is that from?" Marc asked.

"It's the prologue," Chris replied.

"Is there an epilogue?" Marc asked.

Julie leaned forward and snatched the book back from Chris.

"I don't want to know," Julie said. "My dad got it for me as a joke gift. As you all know, I hate scary stuff. I have only skimmed through it so far. But it felt like the perfect book to take on this trip across the Cape."

"So, what kind of stories does it have?" Marc asked.

Julie began flipping through the first few pages of the book. There was an index up front. The legends were all listed alphabetically by the name of the town where the story had occurred. Barnstable. Brewster. Chatham. Eastham. Julie was surprised at how many there were.

"Julie?" Marc asked again.

"Hold, please," Julie answered. "There are lots of different stories here."

Julie got a bit impatient with the index. The titles were not giving her any usable information on each legend. First, she jumped to the one from Truro and read the opening paragraph to herself. Then she tried the one about Sandwich. After skimming that one, she checked out the Chatham story.

"Stop keeping us in suspense," Chris said.

"Well, I am trying to find a really good one."

"Just pick one," Marc said.

"Well, most of them all seem to be the same things. Hauntings. Witches. One is titled 'Drifting from Dennis.' How lame does that sound? I'm trying to find something special."

Julie stopped and spent a minute reading about the one in Truro again. She jumped through a few pages, pausing now and then to skim through a paragraph, to get a feel for what it was about.

"OK, this one is kind of creepy," Julie said. "Plus, it's not far from your condo. The title of the legend is 'The Truro Sausage Factory.'"

"What is that, like some sort of all-male dance show?" Chris asked.

"Sign me up!" Tom said.

"Who doesn't like sausage?" Julie asked.

"What's the story about?" Marc asked.

"Well, there was this guy that would kill people and use the remains of his victims and something called pig tallow to make sausage."

"Sounds yummy to me," Tom said. "Grease and fat should always be on a vacation menu."

"That sounds pretty gross, Julie," Marc said. "Now that you mention it, I'll probably be cooking eggs and bacon for breakfast tomorrow. Or maybe we can get sausage."

"But not with human meat, please," Tom said.

"Want me to read the entire story to you?" Julie asked. "From what I could see there are some disturbing parts to it."

"All of the sausage talk will probably just make me hungry," Marc said. "What else you got?"

"Hold, please," Julie said. She continued to flip through chapters.

Marc reached over and took Chris' hand. She turned and smiled.

"You OK, Babe?" he asked.

"Sure. Just thinking about sausage now."

A full thirty seconds passed as Julie scanned through another legend. Her eyes widened as she read the final paragraph of the story.

"Oh my God!" Julie yelled.

"What?" Tom asked.

"OK, this is it," Julie said. "This is so it! Oh my God! Tom, this is perfect for you. I swear, this is fate!"

"Oh, great," Tom replied. "I can only imagine what you've found."

"OK, so it's called 'Waxed in Wellfleet,'" Julie said. "Legend has it that a family had this local business in town. They made their own candles. But get this ... the wicks were made out of human bone. They would kill people they thought had been disrespectful to them. It was payback. They would carve their bones down to form the wicks.

"It goes on to say that the police never caught them, or figured out where they made the candles. But they found the remains of many of the victims buried in sand dunes out at the beach."

"And why is that fateful for Tom?" Chris asked.

"Because while we're out here this weekend I want to buy my mom a candle for Christmas," Tom replied. "It's the main thing I need to find before we leave. Jewels and I are on a mission."

"Tommy, do you know if she wants one made with human bone?" Marc asked.

Tom laughed.

"I don't know, Julie," Chris said. "That story doesn't seem

that scary, either. I mean, how can you use bones as wicks? That doesn't even make any sense. Can they burn like that?"

"Exactly!" Julie answered. "That's what makes it so scary! It sort of makes my skin crawl. Getting carved up to go into a candle. Gross!"

"Is there more to the story?" Marc asked.

"Oh, sure," Julie said. "Each legend is at least several pages long. Some much longer."

Julie flipped through a few pages and then cleared her throat.

"OK, this is from the very end of the story ...

> All of the remains of the victims had the same terrifying thing in common. The bodies would become unearthed in a sand dune close to the ocean, the waves slowly exposing the horror they had suffered. Their flesh was completely gone. Organs and muscles were missing. The skeletons were completely intact, except for the bones of their fingers and toes. All had been cut clean, as if by a cleaver or machete. Unlike most legends, the victims' bodies were eventually found. These mutilations, and their discovery, were by design. The killers wanted everyone to know the horror and pain they had inflicted, and that they would eventually strike again.

Julie closed the book. The hum of the tires echoed throughout the vehicle. She looked around. Marc's eyes were focused straight ahead on the road. She wasn't sure what Chris was doing. Tom was staring at her with no expression on his face.

"OK, that was fucking creepy," Marc finally said.

"Right?" Julie asked. "Do you want me to read you the entire story?"

"No, Jewels," Tom said. "It said, 'The killers wanted everyone to know the horror and pain they had inflicted, and that they would eventually strike again.' I mean, besides being creepy, it's a total downer."

"So much for entertaining us with something fun," Marc added.

Tom let out a big laugh.

"Well, at least I'm conquering my fears," Julie said. "Let me go look at that sausage story again. Maybe it's less creepy."

"Humans as sausage?" Marc asked. "I think we should just focus on the upcoming weekend. Christmas is a few weeks away."

"All I want for Christmas is some sausage and a candle made from humans," Chris said. "How about you guys?"

Everyone laughed. Chris removed her glasses. She raised them to her mouth to breathe on them, then used the sleeve of her sweater to wipe them clean.

She looked over at Marc and stuck her tongue at him. Marc chuckled. Chris put her glasses back on and looked out the window. The dark clouds that had been hanging over them most of the trip had started to clear.

"I'm starting to think the forecast might be wrong," Chris said. "That storm most likely won't hit us this far out."

Tom unlocked his tablet and waited for the weather app to reload. Chris turned back to watch.

"Are you tethered to your phone?" Chris asked.

"No. I have built-in wireless in addition to Wi-Fi."

"Doesn't that cost extra?"

"Yes, but not much."

"That doesn't make sense."

Marc tensed up. He could sense a battle was brewing. He looked over at Chris, but she was completely focused on Tom. Marc shot Julie a look. She just shook her head.

"Why waste the money when you can just use your phone as a hotspot?" Chris asked.

"Because I like the flexibility. It comes in handy."

"Plus, you had to pay more up front to have that built in. Seems like a total waste of money."

"No, it's not!"

Tom's voice was now raised.

"Guys, guys, guys, enough," Marc said. "Chris, if he wants to spend the money for extra Wi-Fi ..."

"It's not extra Wi-Fi ..." Chris interrupted.

"Whatever it is," Marc continued, "it's his money. Just drop it."

Chris turned and stared out the window. *Once again, he*

does not take my side.

***

Marc checked the fuel gauge. He still had over a third of a tank left. That was plenty. Traffic hadn't been an issue. He had noticed a lot of shops and restaurants had "Closed for the Season" signs hanging in their windows, but all of the gas stations were open.

Marc wasn't sure how much time had passed since the Wi-Fi spat. Miles had gone by in silence. Chris was sulking. Tom was quiet. Julie was disappointed that nobody thought her scary tales were scary. His few attempts at starting a conversation had been met with one-word answers. Marc felt like a dad with three bratty kids.

As they drove along in silence, Julie continued to look through the book. She didn't care what the others thought. The stories were downright disturbing to her. She'd read enough for one day. She closed the book and put it on her lap. She looked over at Tom. He had his face buried in his tablet. Chris was still staring out the side window, purposely turned away from Marc.

"What's the forecast, Tom?" Julie asked, shattering the silence.

Tom had been busy writing an email to his mom to remind her not to spoil Max with any table scraps. He flipped back over to his weather app.

"All of Rhode Island is now under a Blizzard Watch, but most of the Cape is not. About half is under a Warning. We'll know more tomorrow."

"Thanks."

Tom looked over at the book of legends.

"Jewels, what town was the candle legend in?"

"Wellfleet."

"I'm curious ..."

Tom opened his browser and searched for "Wellfleet urban legends." He scrolled and clicked through a few different links, but all he could find were fictional books.

"I'm not finding anything online."

"Try looking out your window," Marc said.

Marc's Ram passed a "Welcome to Wellfleet" sign. He slowed his truck as the highway became a single lane on each side. Julie flipped her book open to the chapter on "Waxed in Wellfleet."

"OK, everyone, this is it," Julie announced. "Time for us to get waxed. Are you ready, Chris?"

Chris turned to look at Julie and shot her a half-smile.

"You mean like a Brazilian wax?" Chris asked.

"Well, for me it would actually be a Colombian wax. That's where my mom is from. Colombia."

"Is there a difference?"

"Yes." Julie paused to think of a good response. "In Colombia, they go all of the way around and do your ass, too."

Chris let out a laugh.

"That's disgusting," Tom said.

"Exactly!" Julie said with a laugh. "Chris, maybe there is a spa somewhere here in town where we can do a two-for-one Colombian waxing!"

"I think it would have to be a three-for-one," Chris replied with a chuckle.

"Three?" Julie asked.

"Well, you said you would get the front and back done. I don't need my ass done. It's naturally smooth back there."

"Oh my God! Stop!" Julie started to belly laugh and snort. "You are making me snort, Becker!"

Chris burst out in laughter at the sound of Julie snorting.

"Hey, Tommy, maybe you should jump up front so we can let these two giggle for the rest of the trip," Marc said.

"Works for me," Tom said. "Besides, I would make a much better co-pilot than Chris."

Chris stopped laughing and turned around to reply to Tom. Marc quickly grabbed her hand to calm her down.

"I'm looking at my navigation app," Tom continued. "I've been monitoring the traffic, and it's going to come to a halt in a few miles. I can reroute you."

"It's fine, Tommy. I know the area you are talking about. There has been construction the past couple of months. It's not a big deal."

"I'm sure I can find a side road somewhere."

"He knows the way, Tom," Chris chimed in.

"But ... "Tom said.

"Relax, Tommy. I've got this. Truro is coming up in the next few minutes. Shut that thing off, will you? Can you just try and enjoy the ride?"

"Enjoy the ride," Chris repeated. She squeezed Marc's hand and smiled. She felt as if Marc had finally taken her side.

Tom shoved his tablet back into his backpack. He turned his attention to the view outside his window. Julie grabbed her book and flipped to the chapter on Truro.

"OK, so Truro has the sausage-maker story," Julie said.

"Babe, I am seriously thinking sausage instead of bacon for breakfast," Marc said. "What do you think? We need to do a grocery run once we get there and unload the truck. If there really might be a storm, the locals will have cleared out a lot of the food."

"That's true," Chris said. "Let me start a list."

Chris popped open the storage bin in the center console. It was a mess. Tons of papers, receipts, napkins, gum, mints. She peered over her glasses and poked around until she found a small notepad and a pen. She shook the pen a few times to make sure the ink was at the tip and tested it in the corner of the pad to make sure it was working. She slid her glasses up to the top of her head so she could see better and wrote "eggs" and "bacon."

"Bacon and eggs," Chris said. "Got it. What else?"

"I have a shopping app on my phone," Tom interjected. "Why don't you let me do the list? The app makes it super easy and you don't waste the paper."

Chris looked up from her list and shook her head.

"I said I would do a list so let me do the list."

"No. My way is better."

Julie punched Tom in the shoulder. He turned and glared at her. She glared back and mouthed the word "Mommy" to him. That was her code word to let Tom know he was acting just like his mother – too controlling. He got the message, although he didn't much like it.

"Never mind," Tom said. "You can do it."

Julie gave Tom a big smile. He just shook his head and turned his attention to the view outside the window.

"I want toast so can you put bread on there?" Julie asked.

"Oh, and Jewels will need peanut butter with that, too," Tom added.

"Oh my God, yes!" Julie said with glee.

"Bad carbs, Julie," Marc replied. "That crap just turns to sugar in your system. And Tommy, peanuts are actually beans. Legumes. Did you know that? They aren't nuts. Beans are inflammatory."

"What's your diet again?" Julie asked.

"No grains, no sugars, no legumes, no dairy, and no processed foods," Marc replied.

Tom and Julie turned to each other at the same time and rolled their eyes.

"No fun, either," Julie said. "He has you eating that shit too, Chris?"

"Since mid-summer," Chris replied. "It actually works great. I've dropped over an inch off my waist."

"I thought you were looking hotter than usual," Julie said. "But if it means no toast and peanut butter I have to pass. Can we at least get cheese?"

"If you insist," Marc said. "Let's just try and get the non-processed kind. Maybe a nice, raw, aged goat cheese."

Chris added cheese to the list.

After several miles, and endless debating over healthy versus processed food, everyone finally came to an agreement on the shopping list. Chris started to read out the grocery list one last time to make sure everyone was on board. Marc interrupted her before she could finish.

"And there it is," Marc announced.

Chris looked up from her list and pulled her glasses down from the top of her head. Tom and Julie leaned forward to look out the front window. They were nearing the part of Route 6 where the views were wide open to the ocean. The sand dunes were low along this stretch and the road faced northwest toward the mainland. On clear days, you could see Plymouth in the distance. But the most spectacular view was of Provincetown, dead ahead. There, roughly six miles away, stood the huge Pilgrim Monument.

The monument was built in the early 1900s and stood over 250 feet tall. Made of solid granite, it commemorated the first landing of the Pilgrims in 1620. It was a bit of a tourist attraction. The four friends had climbed up the inside of the monument earlier this year when Marc first came to the Cape to look for a condo. The views from the top were amazing.

Tom smiled when he saw the monument. He marveled at the way the sand dunes dropped off and gave a striking view of the monolith, towering over everything around it. It was a giant marker, like a stake in the ground that indicated you'd reached your destination. Truth be told, Provincetown – or P-Town as it was often called – was indeed the end of the line. It was the very tip of the Cape. Route 6 came to an end just near the sand dunes of Herring Cove Beach, roughly two-and-a-half miles past the monument.

The skies on the far end of the Cape were mostly cloudy with a few streaks of pale blue showing through. It was approaching 4 p.m. The sun would be setting within the hour. Looking west, there was nothing but dark clouds over the mainland. The sea stretched out in front of them. The ocean water was a sheet of dark gray with ripples of whitecaps popping up near the shoreline.

Tom cracked his window open briefly to inhale the air. It blasted into the truck with a fierce, bitter blow. The cold was shocking. But the sweet scent of sea, salt, and sand quickly filled the truck's cabin.

"Tom!" Julie yelled. "That's cold!"

"No, it's fantastic!" Tom said. "I love the smell of the ocean."

He quickly closed the window and pressed his nose up against the glass. They were passing the row of Days Cottages in North Truro. These tiny, iconic cottages were some of the most photographed and painted in the area. There were almost two dozen of them. They were identical in size, shape, and color. Whenever Tom saw them, he always thought of the game Monopoly and the little plastic houses that you would line up one by one right next to each other. Although he had never stayed in one, just like the sight of the monument, Tom knew that seeing the cottages meant it was just a few more minutes before they would be downtown and most likely at Marc's new condo.

Marc eased off the accelerator as the big silver Ram rolled past the town line dividing North Truro from Provincetown. They passed a weathered painted sign that showed fishermen pulling their daily catch in from their boat as a seagull watched over them.

It read: "Welcome to Provincetown."

SIX

Tradition

Sara stood in the doorway of her family barn, afraid to step inside. The afternoon sun was strong, but the cold winter air blasted across the back of her coat. The large metal table in the middle of the barn was drenched in blood and flesh. She remained frozen as she watched her mother grab a large cleaver from the end of the table.

"I'm here, Mother," Sara said softly.

"Don't be afraid," Mother said. "You need to come in here."

Sara took a few steps in and closed the heavy wooden door behind her. She shoved her hands into her pockets and approached her mother with caution.

Mother took the cleaver and began to run it across a whetstone. Sara watched as her mother methodically ran the blade back and forth, keeping it at the proper angle required to sharpen the edge.

"You need to pay attention," Mother said. "You need to learn."

After several strokes, Mother tested the blade by running it across the tip of her finger. She smiled as the edge easily pierced her skin.

"Have you been practicing your sharpening skills?" Mother

asked.

"Yes, Mother."

Mother wiped the cleaver across her blood-soaked apron and looked at the large cow leg resting on the table. She gripped the hoof with her gloved hands and dragged it closer toward her. Her petite sized masked the strength she possessed. The stainless-steel tabletop became smeared with blood.

"You should go get an apron," Mother said.

Sara walked to the back of the barn to grab one of the aprons hanging on the hooks in front of the stalls. All of the stalls were empty except for one. The cow in the middle pen took a few steps forward to greet her. She stared into the cow's huge almond-colored eyes and ran her hand across its forehead.

"You really should not be watching this, Daisy," Sara said. She put the apron on and returned to her mother's side.

Mother raised her arm up and, with a quick blow, shattered the bone just above the cow's tarsal joint. Sara winced at the sound of the bone cracking beneath the blade of the cleaver.

"Jumpy, are we?" Mother asked. "I know what happened at the store was awful. Your leg will heal. As will your nerves. It just takes time. Right now, I need you to focus on the task at hand."

Mother passed the cleaver to her daughter, who hesitated as she took the tool into her hands. She stepped behind her daughter and pushed her closer to the table.

"You need to learn," Mother said. "It's what we do. This house and barn don't magically pay for themselves. You can't just wave a wand and make your problems simply disappear. Besides, I won't be around forever."

"I know, Mother," Sara said. She turned to face her mother. "It's just harder than I thought it would be."

"Let go of what happened at the store. You should be proud of yourself for surviving that attack. What if you had died?"

"But, Anna ..."

"Anna paid the price. We all must pay at some point."

Sara glanced back at the carcass lying on the floor.

"I know, Mother."

55

Mother tilted her head up and kissed her daughter on the cheek.

"You are so much like your father," Mother said. "He loved these animals too."

Sara managed a slight smile as she thought of her father.

"You get way too attached and forget that these creatures are here to serve us," Mother said. "They aren't here to be your friends. Remember, everything has a purpose. Including our cows. No more delays. Back to work. I still have a lot to teach you."

Mother grabbed her daughter by the shoulders and spun her around. Sara looked down at the huge cow leg and sighed.

"What did I tell you?" Mother asked.

"In times like these, we all have to make sacrifices."

"That's my girl."

Sara raised the cleaver and thrust it down hard into the muscle of the thigh. The blade cut deep into the flesh and lodged itself into the bone. She wiggled the handle to extract the knife.

"Again," Mother said.

Sara released another blow into the cow's leg.

"Faster!" Mother yelled.

Sara followed her mother's instructions and began to chip away at the animal's giant leg. Each blow cut harder and deeper into the beast's flesh.

The blood-soaked blade in Sara's hand brought back visions of last week's attack in the store. Her wounded leg immediately began to throb. Sara did her best to push those memories aside and remain focused on her work. After several violent thrusts, the tibia separated.

"That's my girl," Mother said with pride.

Sara took a few steps back from the table. Mother took the cleaver from her daughter's hand and wiped it across her apron.

"We have a lot more to do," Mother said.

Sara looked across the table at the huge cow carcass slumped on the barn floor. Her eyes began to well up. She turned away and stared at the stalls along the back of the barn. Daisy was looking back at her. Sara felt like she was being judged, and looked away.

Each stall had a small hand-painted sign nailed above the opening. The pen with "Daisy" hanging above it was the only one that wasn't empty. Sara's eyes filled with tears as she looked at the vacant pen next to Daisy. The sign above it read: "Anna."

SEVEN

Provincetown

Marc slowed and made a hard left turn down a long, wide, sloped driveway. There were two signs at the top of the entrance. One read "Exclusive Offering" with the name and number of the developer. A banner across the bottom read "6 Units Left." The number "6" had been recently added. When Marc was here two weeks ago, there had been seven. The other was a huge wooden sign with the name of the complex – "Seabreeze Village."

The look of the sign was similar to the one that marked the entrance to Provincetown. That was by design. The developer mimicked the same thick wood frame and painted seascape of that sign for use in his new development. But instead of a boat and fishermen, the Seabreeze sign had a simple image. The lower half was a tan beach shoreline, and the top half was a deep blue ocean with lighter blue sky at the top. The words "Seabreeze Village" were painted in bright white across the center of it. The heavy sign was almost four feet wide and swung freely from two large hooks attached to an inverted L-shaped support beam. The support beams were stained a weathered dark gray to match the wood frame of the sign.

Once they got to the bottom of the entrance, Marc swung

left in front of a big tree and then circled around it, cranked the wheel left again, and slowly backed the big truck up to the front of the first townhouse in the complex. The ground was covered in crushed stone. There were no painted lines for any sort of parking spaces. But that really didn't matter, since Marc's truck was the only vehicle in the entire complex, aside from a small white work van and a huge black Ford Expedition that Marc recognized as the developer's SUV.

"Well, here we are!" Marc announced.

Seabreeze Village was a relatively new development in Provincetown. New developments were rare due to the finite amount of land that was available for construction. The developer had bought a very old development and then leveled it completely. He then set out to create a unique space. The complex was divided into three sets of four townhomes, for a total of twelve units. They were built in a "U" shape at the bottom of the driveway. Each unit was a two bedroom two and a half bath townhome. All had covered porches in the front, and open patios in the rear.

Marc had Unit #1 on the first corner. He had wanted one of the four corner units away from the driveway. Unfortunately, those were the first to be sold, so he chose one of the two corner units near the entrance. It was a fairly quiet area, since the complex was not adjacent to a busy road. The front of the unit faced west, and he shared his southern wall with Unit #2. The exposed north wall did not get much sun, but he had a large backyard, and overall, he was pleased with his choice.

Marc had big plans for the backyard space behind the patio deck. Due to the slope of the driveway, the backyard area was quite private. He was considering planting a small garden.

All four doors on the truck popped open at nearly the same time.

"Oh! My! God!" Julie shrieked as she leaped from the truck. "It's adorable!"

"Marc, this is awesome," Tom added.

Marc beamed. The past three months had felt like three years, trying to get the work on the townhome completed.

"Thanks, guys. Hey, let me run over to see John, the developer. I'll be right back. Chris, can you loosen the straps and tarps for me? Make sure nothing flew out on the way here."

"Sure thing," Chris said.

Marc headed toward the big black Ford on the far side of the courtyard. He could see the front door to Unit #10 was open. He assumed that's where he would find John.

Chris started to undo the tie-down straps on the Ram. Tom and Julie took a few moments to look around the complex. Julie pulled out her phone and snapped pictures. It was a broad open space. The standout feature was the huge American Holly tree that sat at the bottom of the entrance, dead-center to all twelve units. A wide driveway on the north side of the tree led up the hill to the road. The townhomes were split into three separate groups around the tree. Shooting up over 60 feet tall and almost half as wide, the Holly had obviously been there for a long time. Its tall pyramid shape and huge holly leaves made a striking statement in the open courtyard.

"That tree is incredible," Julie said.

"Marc told me it's an American Holly," Chris explained.

"Wow," Julie said looking at the tree. "They should have named this Holly Village."

"Or maybe Hollywood?" Chris suggested.

"Exactly! Chris, how far are we from town?"

"I think it's only like a five- or ten-minute walk. I have only been out here twice before with Marc. If I remember right, you sort of zig-zag over to Bradford and then Commercial and boom, you're there. Not far from the center of town."

Tom walked over toward the tree and turned back to look at the row of townhomes to which Marc had gone. It really was a beautiful complex. All of it was quintessential Cape Cod architecture. Even down to the wood shaker style shingles and white windows and doors. The nine-panel high-efficiency windows mimicked the wooden windows typically found on older homes. He shivered as a frigid breeze blew, but he felt peaceful. There was complete silence.

As Tom looked around, he noticed about half of the units had small "Sold" signs taped to the front doors. He looked back toward Chris and Julie. They were giggling. Chris was standing up in the back of the truck, and Julie was on the ground pointing and laughing at her. Tom then noticed something incredible in the distance behind them.

"Hey, you can see the monument from here!" Tom said with excitement.

At this time of year, the monument was decorated in long strands of lights that stretched from its peak to the ground. They were anchored several dozen feet away from the base, forming a huge inverted cone. At night, the display could be seen for miles.

"Most definitely, Tommy," Marc said. He had returned from his chat with John and was standing behind Tom.

Tom spun around, a bit startled that he did not hear Marc approaching, even over the crushed stone.

"Did you know that when you bought it?" Tom asked.

"That was one of the reasons I got that unit," Marc answered. "You have fantastic views of the monument from the upstairs bedrooms. They both have huge windows. Especially the master suite that wraps around the corner. Sunrise is amazing. C'mon let me show you."

"Marc!" Chris yelled out as she saw Marc and Tom walking back. "There is a ton to unload. I have the tarps off. Let's move!"

"OK, Babe," Marc replied.

Marc grabbed his keys from the pocket of his tan canvas coat and walked over to the front door. The ring held almost twenty different keys for all of the different properties he was renovating and other investment rental units he owned. Marc fumbled through the giant ring of keys until he found the one for the condo. He unlocked the deadbolt and then the main handle.

"Welcome, everyone," Marc said as he opened the door and stepped inside.

To the left was the spacious kitchen with white cabinets, some with glass doors. There was white subway backsplash tile, and stainless-steel appliances. The countertops were light gray manufactured stone. A big island with four stainless steel pub stools with white leather seats separated the kitchen from the living room. All of the floors were wide-planked wood with a washed-out gray stain. The twelve-foot ceilings on the main floor made the space seem even larger.

"Oh my God. This is gorgeous. Gorgeous!" Julie said. "The furniture is great! This place looks totally finished. I thought you said it was only half done."

"I sort of lied," Marc admitted. "It's completely ready for guests, but I have some custom work I still want to do. Just small finishing touches."

Julie walked by and punched him in the arm.

In the living room was a white leather sectional and a gray-washed wooden table set in the center of it. A large dark gray and white woven area rug completed the look. Off in the corner of the living room was a gray and chrome Barcelona Chair with a small side table and reading lamp. Behind the main living area was a small open den with a fireplace. French doors opened to a patio and private yard. On the other side of the condo was a door that led to the half bath and laundry area.

Opposite the living room and behind the bathroom was the dining area. There was a solid wood dining table, again with the same gray tones as the flooring. The legs, however, were painted white. Two long white leather benches sat on either side of the table.

"What do you think?" Marc asked.

"I feel like I'm in a furniture store," Julie answered. "Or one of those magazines that features fabulous beach homes. This is really amazing!"

"Thanks. I'm really happy with how it came out."

"I think it needs some color," Tom said.

"Seriously, Tom?" Julie asked as she hurried over to the den. "Fireplace! Yay!"

"No, he's right," Marc said. "The walls are completely empty. I plan to get some local art work to add pops of color around the place. The sectional needs some pillows and a small blanket. I'm thinking of either yellows or greens. That's some of the stuff that Chris and I are going to be looking for this weekend. While you two candle shop."

Tom took another look at the kitchen. Something was missing.

"Marc, why didn't you put any handles on the cabinets?" Tom asked.

"You noticed that," Marc said, grinning. "You never miss a thing, do you? John had hooked me up with this supplier out in Wellfleet. The hardware I picked out is unique. Super custom. I ordered them a month ago. That's why I ran over to talk with him. He was supposed to pick them up for me. He didn't. If we have time, I want to run and get them. I brought my tools so I can install them this weekend. Come to think of it, I should have asked John ahead of time. We could have just stopped on the way here today. It totally slipped my mind."

Julie pulled her phone out and took a few pictures of the rooms. Marc walked back to the front door and motioned to Chris to walk with him to the truck.

"Let's start getting this stuff unloaded," Marc said. "We don't have a ton of daylight left. We can get it all piled up inside against the back wall by the stairs. Then we can do a grocery run to get dinner started. We can worry about getting everything unpacked over the next couple of days."

"Sounds good," Chris said.

Chris jumped up into the back of the truck and passed Marc the plastic bins that had everyone's luggage inside. Marc ran them over to the front door and stacked them at the entrance. Tom and Julie came out and started to bring them into the condo. Marc turned back, and Chris handed him the old green metal candle she had taken from the backyard. Marc laughed.

"You packed the candle?" Marc asked.

"Well, you said to go get the table and chairs out back, and it was on the table so I figured you would want it."

"I didn't, but thank you."

Marc took the candle and two of the chairs and headed around toward the side of the townhouse. He passed Tom on the way.

"What can we do to help?" Tom asked.

"Grab a box or a bin and just toss it inside near the stairs. Everything is labeled by room if you want to stack them all together."

"You? Organized?" Tom joked.

"Chris helped."

Tom ran back over to the pickup truck. Chris was in the bed pushing stuff back toward the tailgate. Tom looked at all of the boxes and bins. They were all labeled, just as Marc had said, but he had to spin some of them to read the labels.

"Marc should have loaded all of these in so that the labels faced out," Tom said. "It would have made unloading faster."

Chris bristled, but said nothing. She picked up a large bin filled with sheets and towels and walked to the back of the truck. When Tom reached up to take it, Chris dropped the bin into his arms. Tom stumbled back.

"A little warning next time?" Tom asked, irritated.

"Whoops," Chris said with a smile.

Julie came outside and started taking pictures of Tom and Chris unloading the truck. Marc came up behind her and grabbed her by the shoulders.

"Quick, Marc ... selfie!" Julie yelled. "You know I love my pictures!"

Marc squatted down to Julie's height and wrapped his arms around her waist and lifted her into the air.

"Mind the Girls!" Julie said, giggling. Marc laughed as she fired off a few shots from the camera on her phone. She gave him a quick kiss on the cheek.

"Congrats again," Julie said. "This place totally rocks."

***

It took just over a half-hour for everyone to empty the truck and get the boxes and bins stacked and organized inside the condo. Julie and Tom were now upstairs in the guest bedroom. Their room was the first door at the top of the stairs. Because it shared a wall with the next-door unit, it only had one window. But the window it did have was a large arched window that overlooked the back of the condo. It was recessed in the alcove above the staircase and stood almost five feet tall. It sat only a foot off the floor.

It was a very large bedroom. There were two full-sized beds separated by a small chest of drawers. One bed was next to the giant window, the other at the opposite end near the entrance to the bathroom.

"Jewels, do you mind if ..."

"No, you can have the bed next to the bathroom," Julie answered.

"You know me. Tiny tanks. Especially when I drink vodka."

"It's fine. Besides, that gives me the bed next to the window. I love watching snow fall. Will I get the sunrise there in the morning?"

Tom walked toward the far end of the room and dropped his carry-on and knapsack onto the bed near the bathroom.

"Yes. Marc said the sunrise view up here was amazing."

Julie inspected the huge window and realized it did not have any blinds or curtains on it.

"Shit," Julie sighed.

"I can take that bed if you want me to. I have my sleeping mask."

"No, it's fine. I'll just sleep buried under the blankets."

"It shouldn't be too bad, Jewels. With a blizzard coming, we won't see the sun for the rest of the weekend."

Julie took her heavy duffle bag and kicked it over into the alcove in front of the giant window.

"Be careful with the floor!" Tom said.

"Relax, it has wheels."

Tom shook his head. He wondered if Marc had made the materials throughout the condo Jewels-proof.

"Well, at least be sure to tuck it away in that alcove. I don't want your drunk ass falling all over it in the middle of the night."

"Right?" Julie said, giggling.

Tom began to unpack his clothes and put them into the top drawer of the small dresser between the beds.

"What are you doing?" Julie asked.

"What? Did you want the top drawers?"

"We're only here for two nights. Why are you unpacking?"

"You aren't?"

"No, it's way easier to just pick through my stuff. We'll be on our way home before you know it."

"OK, well, you can live in disarray."

"And you can live overly structured."

They both laughed.

"I really can't get over how gorgeous this place is," Julie said. "She really lucked out."

"Chris?" Tom asked.

"Yes, Chris. She bagged the hottest guy in town. I bet she had no idea how successful Marc was. I can only imagine what this place cost. Real estate here is through the roof. Did Marc tell you what he paid?"

"I didn't ask."

"I think Marc has way more money than we think," Julie said with a grin.

Tom continued to unpack, grouping everything together so it would be easy for him to find what he needed.

"Earlier today you said it probably won't last with them," Tom whispered. Chris and Marc were still downstairs, but he didn't want them to hear him. "They weren't really fighting during the drive out here. Do you really think they might break up soon?"

"Hopeful, are we?"

"What's that supposed to mean?" Tom asked.

Julie walked past Tom carrying her toiletry bag and went into the bathroom.

"Because, Tom, now I'm starting to think that deep down you really *are* jealous."

Tom stood speechless as Julie closed the bathroom door.

***

Marc was unpacking the kitchen boxes. There were over a dozen boxes and bins piled against the back wall. It was going to take a long time to go through all of it, but that could wait. For tonight, he just needed the basics to cook dinner. Chris was upstairs in the master suite taking a shower.

Marc had made his way through two boxes when Tom walked into the kitchen, tablet in hand.

"Marc, I'm trying to find your Wi-Fi connection," Tom said.

"Sorry, Tommy. I don't have internet yet ... or phone ... or TV." Marc chuckled as he thought about everything he still needed to do. "All I have wired up and running is the power."

"Really?"

"It just wasn't a priority for me. Not this trip anyway. All of the lines are run. I just have to activate it. I didn't think to turn any of it on before we came out. Besides, I thought you didn't need that for your tablet."

"Oh, I don't. But the signal is kind of weak here. We are sort of down in this little valley at the bottom of the driveway. It's fine. I was just asking."

"When is dinner?" Julie yelled from upstairs.

"Oh, shit. We need food," Marc said to Tom. "Hey, you want to take a ride with me to the grocery store? Chris is in the shower and she takes forever."

"Sure thing."

Marc grabbed the grocery list Chris had made and shoved it into his pocket.

"Hey, Julie!" Marc yelled up to her. "Tommy and I are doing a food run. Can you let Chris know? We won't be gone long."

"Get bread!" Julie yelled back.

It was dark now, just after 6 p.m. The huge courtyard only had a single source of light, a pair of landscape lights located at the top of the driveway that pointed up to illuminate the Seabreeze Village sign.

Marc switched on the light for the front porch as they exited the townhouse. It did a good job of lighting up the entrance, but cast very little light beyond that.

All of the surrounding units were pitch black, save for the orange glow of the tiny lights on the doorbells at each front door. Tom looked up at the massive American Holly tree. What was once so beautiful in the daylight was now a black spire, swaying and creaking in the wind.

Clouds had moved in, completely concealing the stars. On a clear night, the stars in Provincetown were very bright. The tip of the Cape was so far from huge city lights that the night sky was normally a canvas of black velvet speckled with tiny diamonds. Tonight, however, the sky reminded Tom of the dark gray sea they had driven past a few hours ago.

"They really need to get some lights down here," Tom said as he opened the door on the Ram.

"It's on John's punch list. Some really nice lampposts are

going in next month. He also wants to install some lighting on that giant Holly. Maybe I'll toss a higher-watt bulb in my outdoor lights for now."

The two of them jumped into Marc's truck and began the short drive over to the grocery store.

***

"Where is everyone?" Chris asked as she descended the staircase. She looked stunning in a pair of dark indigo jeans and a form-fitting black sweater.

Julie had lined up four martini glasses in a row on the kitchen island, alongside a shaker and a bottle of vodka.

"They went to get groceries. Cocktails?"

"Like you have to ask. Allow me."

Chris grabbed a few ice cubes from the freezer along with some olives from the fridge. Julie watched in amazement as Chris whipped up a pair of dirty martinis.

"Cheers!" Chris said with a smile. She pulled out one of the barstools and sat down next to Julie.

Julie took a sip of the drink and winced.

"Damn, that's strong," Julie said. "But oh, so good."

Julie glanced over at the stainless-steel refrigerator. It was obviously very high-end. The upper half was a split French door design with a pull-out freezer on the bottom.

"Hey, Chris, I know I'm being nosey, but what did Marc pay for this place?"

Chris took a long sip from her martini glass.

"I forget."

"You're a realtor. How could you forget? Property out here is through the roof. And this is just a vacation place for him. Aren't you the least bit curious?"

"This is his project, not mine," Chris said, dismissing the conversation.

Julie studied Chris' face for a moment, but there was no sign of excitement that her boyfriend had spent a minor fortune on a vacation home. In fact, she didn't appear to care at all. She was completely engrossed in her martini glass. Julie got the hint.

"OK, so let's figure out tomorrow," Julie said, changing the subject. "Tom and I need to go find that stupid candle for his mom. Trust me. You and Marc don't want to get dragged along on that treasure hunt. Besides, it sounds like you two still have lots of stuff to get for this place. I was thinking we should plan to meet for lunch someplace in town."

"That works for me. But I honestly don't know what Marc needs to get."

Chris had already chugged down half her martini. She reached over and grabbed the shaker to top off her drink.

"So, Julie, what's the deal with this candle you have to find for Tom's mom? Is it really important or something?"

"The candle isn't important. It's making sure it is exactly what she wants, or Tom will get shit for it."

"I've never met her, but she sounds like a real control freak. Worse than Tom."

"She's not a bad person. She adores Tom. She means well. She just relies on him for everything. For too much, if you ask me. But I get it. I mean … It's just the two of them. You know that Tom's dad died when he was like twelve years old, right?"

"Oh, I didn't know that."

"I thought you knew. Shit. Well do me a favor and don't ask him about it."

"Why?"

"His dad's death is a topic he won't discuss. You will completely set him off."

"Why?"

Julie paused to take a sip from her drink.

"Tom … Tom was there when his dad got killed."

"Holy shit. At twelve? So … like … what did he see? How did he die? An accident?"

"No, Chris. His dad … his dad was murdered."

Chris and Julie stared at one another in silence.

"Tom saw his dad murdered?" Chris asked. "Holy shit! What … what happened?"

"He's never told me the details. All I know is he was there. He saw the whole thing."

"At twelve? Wow. Do you think that's why … why …"

"Stop! Shit. I knew I shouldn't have said anything. No more

questions. And you can't ask him about it, Chris! He will rip me apart for telling you!"

"OK! OK! I can't imagine ... What ... what does that do to you?"

"No more questions, Chris. And do not discuss it with him. Promise me!"

"I promise, Julie. Fuck."

Julie spun around and walked away from the island.

"Now I'm stressed."

Julie started going through the kitchen cabinets, in the hope of finding some chips or crackers. She knew food would help to calm her. The cabinets, unfortunately, were bare.

"OK, so after that did his mom overcompensate because the dad wasn't there?" Chris asked. "Did she coddle him?"

"It was just the opposite. Tom had to become the man of the house. At twelve years old. The problem is that his mom is a perfectionist. She rode him hard, always correcting him. Maybe she was overcompensating. Who knows. Tom, unfortunately, has turned out a lot like his mom."

Chris noticed Julie still seemed a bit stressed.

"So that's why he can be such an annoying little fucker."

Julie turned to look at Chris and noticed she was grinning.

"Totally," Julie replied. She managed a chuckle. "I love him to death, but he can definitely get on my nerves. I have a code word I use with him."

"Really?"

"Yes, when he is getting out of control, I get his attention and mouth the word 'Mommy' to him. It shuts him right up."

"That's hilarious."

"Yes and no. I mean, I hate having to do that, you know? He gets so controlling and bossy. I just wish he would unwind. He needs to enjoy the ride. Like Marc told him to on the way out here. Marc sees it, too."

Chris paused for a bit and stared down into her martini glass. It was half-empty again.

"Marc gets frustrated that Tom and I are always getting into arguments," Chris said.

"Really?"

"He thinks we are both too competitive or something."

"Well, in some ways I can sort of see it. I mean, you are both ... stubborn."

Julie noticed Chris was more than halfway through her second drink. Julie was less than a quarter done with her first one. She checked the martini shaker and it was almost empty. She decided to top it off and poured in more vodka and olive juice, along with lots of ice.

"He just gets on my nerves. I hate being told what to do. I always have."

Chris took another long sip from her drink. She placed it on the counter and looked up at Julie.

"Growing up, my dad was always super strict," Chris continued. "He has this plumbing business. It's a family business. My mom does all of the accounting and manages all of the finances. He wants me to one day take over for my mom. My brother is all onboard to take over the actual plumbing side of things. With my dad, it's all about carrying on the family name and business. But I have no interest in being an accountant. I hate math!

"We fought about it all of the time. I could not move out fast enough. Once I was twenty-one, I was gone. I moved in with friends and got a bartending job. I saved my money and took the classes that I needed to in order to get my real estate license.

"My dad and I have a very strained relationship. He wants me to fail. Can you believe that? He keeps telling me it's only a matter of time before I give up and come back to the family business. When I moved into my own apartment this summer, he told me not to bother unpacking because I wouldn't be able to afford it for long."

"I'm so sorry," Julie said.

"Thanks. Look, it's not that Tom is always right or thinks that he's right. It's that he is always correcting me. Always telling me what to do. Annoys the shit out of me. Marc does it, too."

"Marc is always correcting you?"

"No, Marc is always ..."

Chris slid her empty glass across the island. Julie filled her glass from the shaker, and passed it back. She also grabbed two plastic cups off the counter and filled them with filtered water from the fridge. She put one down in front of Chris, hoping she would pace herself.

"I feel like Marc is always telling me what to do. He's always trying to define my future. Like my dad."

"How?"

"Well, look at this condo. He keeps talking about this place being for us. Us!"

"And that's a bad thing? Look at this place! Look at Marc! He's a major catch. Do you know how lucky you are?"

"I know I should feel that way," Chris said. She let out a deep sigh. "But I don't. Marc is talking about how over the next few years he can start to build out his business here in town, to expand it. Some partnership thing with the developer here. I don't really know. He thinks I should plan to get my Massachusetts real estate license so that we can start to work together both in Providence and here in Provincetown. I find us the homes and he has the resources to buy and flip them."

"What's wrong with that plan?"

"We haven't even been together a year yet, Julie. Marc is great. Really, he is. But the constant pressure he puts on defining us ... defining me ... It just pushes me away. I get enough of that shit from my family. I don't want to go into business with my family. Or Marc!

"My focus right now is on building up a clientele in Providence and then getting to the point that I can start my own real estate company. That's my five-year plan. It always has been. And I don't really know where Marc fits into all of that. Marc has helped me advance my real estate business big time. He truly has. For that I am thankful. But ... he and I in business together? And also dating? I think maybe the timing is just wrong, you know? This is all too soon for me."

"What does Marc have to say about all of this?"

Chris hesitated and enjoyed another sip from her glass.

"I'm not big on sharing my feelings."

"Look, I may not have the best track record with men, but I do know you have to communicate. I'm sure if you talked things through he would understand and maybe even back off. Be more supportive. Find a way to make things work short-term for a better long-term."

They both looked up at the front window as the Ram pulled up to the front of the townhouse, the headlights beaming in through the kitchen window. Chris took a long sip from her martini and placed the glass back on the counter.

"The thing is, Julie, I don't know that I want a better short-term. You know we had a huge fight after that stupid game night. What you don't know is I told him I was done. For good. Marc begged me to come back. Daily! I'm here this weekend to help him set this place up. I keep my promises. He is still holding out hope for us. I just ... I just don't know. Honestly, deep down, I'm ready to move on."

The front door cracked open as Marc and Tom returned. The wind pushed the door open. Tom quickly reached out to stop it from slamming against the backstop. He was carrying three large brown paper bags with both arms. Marc had a huge amount of food, with three big plastic bags in each hand. They spread all of the bags out on the main counter in the kitchen.

Tom tossed the crumpled grocery list onto the kitchen island toward Chris. He and Marc took off their jackets and hung them on the coat hooks in the hallway.

"My shopping app would have been better," Tom said. "The store was mobbed due to the blizzard. We couldn't get all the stuff on the list."

Marc slid a bottle of champagne onto the kitchen island and grabbed four plastic cups.

"I see you two are already deep into the booze," Marc said. "I don't have champagne flutes yet. So, we can use these cups. Julie, can you get your phone and set up for a self-timer?"

Marc popped the bottle of champagne open and poured it into the four plastic cups. Julie propped her phone up against the back wall of the kitchen counter and set it for a ten second delay. Everyone gathered on the opposite side of the island. Marc and Chris were on the ends. Tom and Julie were squeezed into the middle sitting up high on the bar stools.

"A toast everyone," Marc said. "To the first of many great adventures here."

Everyone leaned forward and held their red cups together just as the flash went off. Julie did not bother to take a sip. She ran around to the other side and checked the photo.

"Oh my God, it's perfect!" Julie said.

***

Chris, Marc, and Julie were lounging on the sectional as Tom washed the pans from dinner in the kitchen sink. Marc had prepared a fantastic meal, even if the main course was a rotisserie chicken from the market. Marc made three different vegetable dishes to go with the chicken. Julie had begged for rice or bread, but Marc had skipped those. He was already anxious about the sugar used to prepare the chicken. The clock said 10 p.m.

"Tommy, are you up for the gym tomorrow?" Marc asked. "Chris and I will be up with the roosters."

"Sure," Tom replied, knowing he had no intention of going.

"Hey, when we get back home I want you to do another kickboxing session with me," Marc said. "I didn't bring my gloves, so we can't do that this weekend. But when we get back, I want you to try again."

"Tom, you never told me you tried kickboxing," Julie said. She had been reading her book of legends but paused to listen in on the conversation.

"Because I sucked. It was stupid," Tom said. He began drying the pans he had stacked up.

"Why do you say that?" Marc asked.

Tom turned around to face the living room. Julie was stretched out on one side of the sectional facing the dining room. She had pulled her hair up into a bun and had secured it with a big elastic wrap. Chris had passed out in the wedge of the corner of the sectional. Marc was reclined along the opposite side, facing the kitchen.

"I felt like everyone at the gym was watching us," Tom answered. "I mean, you outweigh me by like seventy or eighty pounds and probably eight inches in height. I could never kick your ass. Everyone at the gym was staring, probably laughing at the David versus Goliath show. It was embarrassing."

"Size doesn't matter, Tommy."

"I would beg to differ," Julie teased.

Marc tossed a crumpled napkin across the coffee table and hit Julie on her head. She brushed it away and returned to focus on her book.

"Ignore her," Marc continued. "Sure, in total hand-to-hand combat you would think we aren't evenly matched. But you have speed on your side. All you need to do is get one good hit in and you can take anyone down. You were good on the attack, but you retreated when it came to defense. You can't always run away."

Tom turned back toward the sink and stared out the window.

"So, are you a certified instructor?" Julie asked. She put her book aside and looked across the coffee table toward Marc.

"I'm not," Marc replied. "I just enjoy it. I took lessons weekly for a few months last year. It's a great full-body workout."

"Maybe you can teach me when we get back?" Julie asked. "I know everyone thinks I'm a badass, but I hit like a girl."

"I'd be happy to. But Tommy, you need to do it, too. It builds confidence. Fight or flight, buddy. You need to work on your fight."

Tom continued to gaze out the front window. Beyond Marc's truck he could see the base of the large American Holly tree standing tall in the darkness of the night. He desperately wanted this conversation to end.

"Chris, wake up," Marc said. He gave her a slight shove with his foot.

"What?" Chris asked.

"We need to get to bed, Babe. Long day tomorrow."

"What time is it?" Chris asked. "Aren't we going out bar-hopping?"

"No!" Marc replied. He wasn't sure if she was serious or not.

Chris sat up and noticed Julie stretched out to her left with her face buried in her book. She reached over and started to tickle Julie's foot. Julie recoiled.

"Oh my God!" Julie screamed. "You scared the shit out of me!"

"Good!" Chris laughed.

"It's not funny! I was reading the legend about the candle

killer. The one in Wellfleet. It's really fucked up."

"Listen, everyone," Marc said. "Something dawned on me when Tommy and I went to the store. I only have one spare key that I had made for Chris. I eventually want to make extra sets so everyone has one. I'll try and do that tomorrow at the hardware store. We've all got different things to do this weekend. Maybe we can hide the extra key outside somewhere."

"Tom and I can share the extra key, Marc," Julie said. She sat upright and rubbed her now bloodshot eyes. "Don't worry about it."

"But I might have to meet up with the developer tomorrow. Chris won't want to deal with that, so then Chris might be without a key. You guys could end up texting each other all day trying to meet up to get back in here. Julie, you may get tired of candle-shopping and want to come back early."

"Whatever you think is best," Julie replied. "We can figure it out in the morning."

"We can put it under that old candle," Chris said. "The green metal one I brought from your house. You set it up out back, right? The little patio set."

"Yes," Marc answered. "It's on the table out back."

"So, let's do that," Chris said. "We just need to remind Julie tomorrow because she's too drunk to remember."

"Remember what?" Julie asked. She pulled the elastic from her hair and shook her bun out. "That the key is under the candle?"

"Right," Chris said.

"The key is under the candle," Julie repeated. "Got it. See, you are the drunk one, not me. You probably already forgot."

"Forgot what?" Chris asked.

Both Chris and Julie started to giggle. Marc stood up and headed to the kitchen. Chris and Julie were silly enough sober. He knew where this tit-for-tat was headed.

"The key is under the candle!" Julie laughed.

The laugh quickly turned into a belly laugh. Chris was determined to get a snort out of her.

"What's under the candle?" Chris asked.

"Oh my God! Stop!" Julie laughed and then finally snorted.

"The fucking key!"

"So now it's a fucking key?" Chris laughed. "A key to fuck with? Or be fucked by?"

Marc walked up behind Tom. Chris and Julie were still going back and forth about the key being under the candle. Tom had been staring out the window, oblivious to the antics in the living room.

"Thanks for doing all the dishes, Tommy," Marc said.

Tom did not turn around. He changed his focus from the holly tree outside to the pane of glass on the window. He could see Marc's reflection as he towered over him.

"Happy to help," Tom replied.

"You OK?"

"Sure. Just thinking."

"About?"

"Stuff."

Marc let out an audible sigh. Between Chris and Tom, he wasn't sure which one was the tougher nut to crack open. He rested his hands on Tom's shoulders and squeezed lightly.

"Such as?" Marc asked.

Tom looked down into the sink. There were several small puddles of water across the bottom. He grabbed a towel next to the sink, and wiped them dry.

"Just ... stuff," Tom answered without looking up. "I'm just tired. Long day. Lots of booze. Thanks again for the great dinner."

"Anytime, Tommy."

Tom draped the damp towel over the handle of the dishwasher. He turned and walked around Marc. He did not want to lock eyes with him. Tom noticed Chris and Julie sitting on the sectional laughing hysterically. He didn't know why. He just needed to get to bed.

EIGHT

Holiday Shopping

The door to the guest bedroom swung open. The light from the window in the alcove next to Julie's bed had already filled the room. Chris stood in the doorway and looked back and forth between the two beds. Julie and Tom were both fast asleep.

Julie's bed was closest to the door. She had a white cotton blanket completely covering her head to block the light from the window. All Chris could see were sections of her long brown hair peeking out from the top of the blanket. She was snoring. Chris wondered how she could be breathing with her face completely covered.

At the opposite end of the room, Tom was curled up in a little ball with his arms wrapped around one of the pillows. He had his back to the door and was facing the bathroom.

"Wake up!" Chris screamed at the top of her voice.

Julie jumped and sat upright, her disheveled hair partially covering her face.

"Oh my God, Chris!" Julie yelled. "What the hell time is it?"

Julie looked around the room. No clocks. She searched for her phone.

"It's 8:15. Marc and I just got back from the gym. Why the

hell are you two still in bed?"

"Because it's Saturday," Tom answered. He rolled over and turned in the direction of Chris' voice, his eyes covered by a sleep mask. "And it's cold out. And it's Saturday."

"Nice mask," Chris said sarcastically.

"Thanks."

"Marc tried to wake you up, Tom. Do you remember?" Chris asked.

"Not really."

"You were completely passed out! It was hilarious. Well, the coffee is brewing, and Marc is getting ready to make breakfast. Any requests?"

"French toast," Julie said. "With ibuprofen sauce."

"Ditto on that, Jewels," Tom said.

"I'll go tell the chef," Chris said. She left the door open and turned to head downstairs.

Julie flung the blanket back over her face and closed her eyes. Tom rolled over and hugged his pillow again, and immediately fell back to sleep.

***

"Good morning, princess," Marc said. "Coffee?"

Julie had finally made her way downstairs, although she wasn't exactly ready to start her day. Her hair was pulled back into a bun, and she was wearing pink and red flannel pajamas and white bunny slippers. The one on her right foot had a mangled ear; the left one was missing an eye. Tom called them her "Zombunnies."

"Yes, please," Julie said as she made her way across the dining room to the kitchen. "Aren't you cold?"

"I'm fine," Marc replied. He was still in his gym clothes - long gray sweatpants, and a tight black tank top. Around his neck was a black leather-cord choker. The choker had a small pewter cross that hung from the end. It rested perfectly just below his Adam's apple. "The Italian in me runs hot."

"Where is the ..." Julie started to ask.

"Ibuprofen is next to the coffee."

Julie smiled when she spotted the big bottle of pills. Marc

MJ Howson

had set two large empty mugs next to the coffee pot along with a selection of sweeteners and a half-pint of French vanilla-flavored creamer. She took one of the mugs and filled it with coffee.

"The store was all out of milk and cream, so I had to get that artificially flavored processed crap," Marc said. "I wasn't sure if that would be OK."

"It's fine. You keep forgetting that when I'm hungover I take my coffee hot and black. Like my men."

Marc laughed.

Tom appeared at the bottom of the staircase and stopped and yawned. He was sporting blue and gray flannel pajama bottoms, a baggy gray long-sleeved t-shirt that looked at least a size too big, and thick, gray woolen socks.

"Hey, sleepy head," Marc said. "You missed the gym."

Tom was carrying his knapsack. He scuffed his feet across the floor as he made his way into the kitchen and tossed the bag onto the sectional as he passed by. His head ached. He was going to need some of that ibuprofen.

"Sorry, Marc."

"It's OK, Tommy."

Marc pulled Tom close as he walked by and tousled his already messy blond hair. Tom gave him a quick one-armed hug before continuing on toward the coffee. Julie was already seated at the island.

"Did you get my request for French toast?" Julie asked.

"Yes, I did," Marc answered. "You have been so tolerant of me and my strict diet. I mean, I denied you your carbs with dinner last night. So yesterday I decided I would do bread for you this morning. As a surprise."

"Really?" Julie asked. She was genuinely shocked.

"Yes. But then we got to the store and they were out of bread. Sorry. Surprise!"

Julie glared at Marc. She knew that wise-ass grin. He had never planned to get her bread.

"You are testing my limits, Sirola. Especially hung over."

Tom filled the last remaining mug with coffee and added the flavored creamer. He left the mug on the counter and walked over to the sectional. He picked up his knapsack and

80

dropped it onto the empty stool next to Julie.

"What now?" Julie asked.

"Who loves you?" Tom asked.

"Is that a trick question?" Julie replied.

Tom then proceeded to pull a loaf of cinnamon-raisin bread from his knapsack.

"Oh my God! You do! You love me!"

Julie gave Tom a huge hug and a kiss on the cheek.

"Tommy! Where did you get that from?" Marc asked.

"I brought it from home."

"You little shit!"

"He's the little shit that I love!" Julie said as she flipped Marc the middle finger.

"Well, you can make your own French toast," Marc said.

"No problem. Tom can do that for me. Right, Tom? Or even just plain toast is fine. You know I don't really cook. I'm known for my secret family recipe for boiled water."

Tom reached into his bag again and pulled out a jar of peanut butter.

"Tommy! What the hell?" Marc said, but now he was laughing.

"What?" Tom asked. "Jewels loves PB and toast in the morning."

"Yay!" Julie exclaimed with glee.

"You two ..." Marc laughed. "The little plotters and schemers. The only problem with your grand plan, Tommy, is that I don't have a toaster."

Tom and Julie stared at each other and then looked around the kitchen.

"Shit," Tom said. "No worries, Jewels. We bought eggs. I'll make us French toast."

"That works for me," Julie said as she reached for a banana from the bunch that was sitting on the island. "Besides, peanut butter goes great with bananas."

***

The long hot shower did wonders to wake Tom up. The ibuprofen had also kicked in, clearing his headache. Julie was lying on her bed, typing on her cell phone. Tom had made the beds while she was in the shower. He frowned as he noticed she was wrinkling his work.

"What are you doing?" he asked.

"Texting with my mom back in New York."

"Everything OK?"

"The usual family drama. My brothers and sisters are all insane. I swear, the best thing I did was to move away to college and never go back. Can you believe I'm the normal one?"

"No."

"Exactly. So, listen, I don't mind helping you find that candle for your mom, but can you try not to obsess about it?"

"Obsess about it?"

"Like I have to spell it out. Look, this is our only full day here. We head back at some point tomorrow afternoon. So let's try and make the most out of it."

"I really don't think it will take that long to find ..."

"To find the perfect gift? Tom, I love you, but for once could you just try and meet your mom halfway? Why spend your entire time away on vacation trying to get something for her? I told you yesterday, get her an LED candle. Or at the very least, if you find something that checks off some of your requirements, then go for that. Compromise."

Marc stuck his head into the room. He had on jeans and a lightweight, dark-green V-neck cashmere sweater. The black leather choker was tight against his olive skin. His pewter cross was positioned perfectly in the center of the V.

"You ready to go?" Marc asked.

Chris stepped around Marc and filled the other half of the doorway, wearing an almost identical outfit as Marc's, except her sweater was a white crewneck.

"Just about," Tom said. "We'll be down soon."

Marc and Chris turned and headed downstairs.

Tom's knapsack was sitting on the floor next to his bed. He looked inside to make sure he had everything -- tablet, charge cords, extra backup power block, and snacks. He tossed the pack over his shoulder, unplugged his cell phone from the wall and slid it into the front pocket of his jeans.

Julie grabbed her purse and they headed downstairs together.

Chris was near the front hallway putting on her leather jacket. Marc was sitting at the dining room table lacing up his construction boots.

"You're bringing your entire knapsack?" Chris asked.

"Why not?" Tom replied. He tossed his bag onto one of the stools at the island in the kitchen.

"It just seems like overkill," Chris said. "Why lug it all over town?"

Marc did not want to wait for an argument to start, so he quickly changed the conversation.

"So, let's figure today out," Marc said. "You two are going on the great candle hunt. Tommy, as much as I would love to spend the day inspecting every gift shop in town to please your mom, I just have too much to do."

"Why don't you just get her a candle online?" Chris asked. "I don't see why ..."

"Chris and I need to hit some of the art galleries over in the east end," Marc said, cutting Chris off. "I also need to connect with John the developer. It's just after 9:30. Why don't we plan to meet somewhere for lunch after one o'clock? That should be plenty of time. If anyone needs more time we have the rest of the afternoon."

"It won't take us long," Julie said. "Everything will probably be closed this time of year."

"Not this weekend, Julie," Marc said. "It's Holly Folly."

"Holly what now?" Julie asked.

"I totally forgot about that!" Tom said. "Marc, you are missing the Jingle Bell Run. Doesn't it start soon?"

"I think it kicks off in an hour. I may be into fitness, Tommy, but there is no way I am running half-naked through town in this freezing weather."

Holly Folly was one of the many events that Provincetown held to help boost tourism during the off-season. Holly Folly took place the first weekend of December. The town scheduled several different events, including brunches and tours. The Jingle Bell Run was a brisk one-mile run through the town center that doubled as a costume party. Some runners would dress as Santa Claus or Mrs. Claus. But most just wore a Santa hat along with a bathing suit and nothing else. Tourists were often taken by surprise when they found themselves suddenly surrounded by Santas in thongs while strolling through downtown.

Julie was already standing by the door ready to head out.

"I hope we get down there in time to see some of the race!" Julie exclaimed. "Meeting up around one should be good. We can text and figure out where to eat. Hopefully, we'll be done candle shopping by then and we can all hang out together the rest of the day. Did anyone check the weather forecast?"

Everyone turned to look at Tom. He smiled.

"P-Town is under a Blizzard Watch. But the Warning now extends all the way out to Sagamore. I think it's only a matter of time before they switch us to a Warning. Providence is already getting hit bad. It's almost under a foot of snow."

"Shit," Chris said. "My car will be buried back home. Glad I parked at the front of your driveway, Marc."

"OK, everyone, then let's definitely try and get as much shopping done as possible before lunch," Marc said. "We can have a nice meal and then come back here and hang out. Maybe light a fire tonight and play some games."

"As long as Chris is up for another ass-whooping," Tom said, smiling.

Marc gave Tom a long stare and shook his head. Chris opened her mouth to make a comment but stopped. She remembered the long talk she and Julie had yesterday.

"Maybe we can find a game better suited for tall people?" Chris said.

"Point to Chris!" Julie laughed. "Oh, wait, that was a dig at me, too!"

Chris laughed as she pulled her gloves out to put them on. Tom walked past her to the fridge and pulled out some bottled waters and tossed them into the back compartment of his backpack, separate from the electronics. He zipped the compartment closed and double-checked everything to make sure all of the pockets were secure. Tom grabbed the bag to toss it over his shoulder but the luggage tag had snagged on the corner of the stool. He quickly freed it and then made his way over to the door.

"OK, so we agree on the plan?" Marc asked.

"Yes," Julie said, growing impatient. "Let's move."

Marc grabbed his huge key ring off of the kitchen counter.

"Did you put the extra key out back?" Chris asked.

"Yes," Marc said. "Chris, make sure we hit the hardware store. You know I'll forget. I want to get those extra keys made."

Chris opened the front door. The wind flung the door hard toward her, as it blasted into the room. She had to catch it before it slammed against the wall. Marc closed and locked the door once everyone was outside. Julie pulled the knit hat her ya-ya had made for her tight over her ears.

"Where is the key, Julie?" Chris asked.

"Isn't it up your ass?" Julie replied with a chuckle. "No, wait, silly me. It's under the candle!"

"The fucking candle," Chris added. "Or is it the fucking key?"

"Either way, one of them is getting fucked."

Julie and Chris immediately started to giggle as they led the way up the driveway. Chris had her hands in her pockets. Julie slid her arm through Chris' left arm, and held on as the wind blew hard against them.

"What candle?" Tom asked.

"Oh my God. Were you not paying attention last night?" Julie asked.

"I guess not."

"Marc only has one extra key," Julie explained. "So we are going to leave it under the candle on the patio table out back. In case anyone needs to come back alone."

"Wow, I seriously thought you were too drunk to remember any of that," Chris said. "Apparently, Tom was more drunk than you. I'm impressed."

"Never underestimate me, Becker."

"So noted!"

"Tommy, if you and Julie try to come back here and get lost, just head over to Shank Painter or Bradford and look for the Seabreeze Village signs," Marc said. "John has them up all over. You can follow them back here."

"No worries, Marc," Tom said. "I have my GPS to find it."

***

"Oh my God ... I am so over this," Julie said.

She and Tom had spent the past two hours walking up and down Commercial Street. Tom's strict requirements for his mother's gift had so far left them empty-handed.

At slightly over a mile long, Commercial Street was the busiest part of Provincetown. It had the bulk of the restaurants, shops, and galleries. With its flat terrain, you could easily walk from one end to the other in about twenty minutes. Many of the popular guesthouses were also along Commercial, or sprinkled along the side streets between Commercial and Bradford Streets.

"What's on Bradford for shops?" Tom asked. "I can't remember."

"I have no clue. I never get out to P-Town."

"Well, now that Marc has that condo, we'll probably be coming here way more."

"True. I predict epic adventures here for all of us. But we haven't had any luck finding you a stupid candle. The only highlight of the morning was getting swarmed by those five really sexy Santas doing the Jingle Bell Run."

Tom laughed.

"Well, we should check out the side streets between here and Bradford, too. There are always more shops to be discovered."

"Sorry, but I'm done," Julie told him. "This is our only full day here in town and I feel like we're wasting it. Besides, I'm getting hungry."

Tom stopped walking. He slid his backpack off his shoulder and unzipped the front compartment to see what he had for snacks.

"I have those little cheese-and-cracker snack packs that you like. Have a snack and we can keep shopping."

"No, I want real food."

"Real food? You mean the super healthy non-processed kind that Marc always eats?"

"Seriously?" Julie asked with a laugh. "No, I mean real food, like a burger and fries. What time is it?"

Tom checked his phone.

"It's just about noon, Jewels. Still a bit early. We aren't supposed to meet Marc and Chris for another hour."

Julie shoved her hand into Tom's knapsack and felt around until she found the package of crackers.

"Didn't you grab water when we left?" Julie asked.

"It's the big pocket in the back."

Julie rummaged around the other pocket and pulled out a bottle of water.

"You drive me crazy sometimes, but without you I would be starving and dehydrated."

Tom laughed as he tightened the zippers on his pack and tossed it back over his shoulder. They continued walking, working their way back to the center of town. Julie pulled off her purple gloves so she could tear open the package of crackers.

"You know what we should be doing?" Julie asked. "We should totally be getting Marc a housewarming gift!"

"That's a great idea. He needs color in that place."

"Marc is very particular on how he designs and decorates. I wouldn't go down that road."

"I'm good with color."

"Yes, but it's not your place. Let him furnish it."

"But I would really like a centerpiece statement thing. Maybe like for the dining room table. Or that big blank wall in the living room."

Julie stopped walking and waited for Tom to turn back. Once they locked eyes she mouthed "Mommy" to him. He frowned.

"We need something else, Tom."

"A toaster?"

Julie laughed.

"Well, that would be more for me than for him with that stupid diet he follows."

"What about a toaster oven?"

"That might work. Do you think we could get one in town?"

Tom looked around to get his bearings.

"I thought there was a kitchen store somewhere. Or that hardware store might sell them, too."

Julie took a long drink from the bottle of water and shoved two more crackers into her mouth.

"I get so lost on this street, Jewels. I'm not sure where they are."

"Hey, we could also get a nice set of champagne flutes," Julie said.

"I like that idea. I'm just not sure where to find them. Want me to search online for local stores?"

The bell atop the Provincetown Town Hall began to ring to signal that it was officially noon. The building had undergone a massive two-year renovation that was completed in late 2010. The refurbishing included updates to the bell assembly at the top of the clock tower. Julie glanced up at the eight-sided cupola as the clanging bell echoed against the surrounding buildings.

"No. My vote is we go find a place with a nice view of the bay. Indoors. Out of this fucking wind. And get a couple of glasses of wine."

"And?"

"And what? Drink them."

Tom laughed.

"Seriously, Tom, we don't have to get him a gift now. I love the idea of champagne flutes more than the toaster oven. They're small, and he can keep them tucked away. He will always remember they are from us. We can get something super nice."

"High-end crystal. Classy."

"That's me!"

***

Tom slid the key into the back patio door of the townhome and spun the lock clockwise. The wind along the back of the development was strong because of the gulley they were in. He held the doorknob, letting the wind push the door open. Julie walked around him to escape the cold. Tom put the key back under the green metal citronella candle on the small patio table and quickly followed her into the living room.

Inside the condo was toasty warm. Marc had set the heat to 70 before they left that morning. Julie bumped it up to 72. The wind outside had continued to pick up as the day had progressed. The temperature had dropped to 37 degrees. The wind chill made it feel below 30.

Julie pulled her hat off, immediately sending her hair into a static mess. She tossed the hat onto the coffee table, along with her purple gloves, and flopped onto the sectional so she could pull her boots off. Tom headed to the front door to hang his coat. On his way, he dropped his knapsack next to Julie on the sectional.

Marc and Chris had ended up meeting them for cocktails at 12:30. That turned into a nearly two-hour lunch. Marc had found a few pieces of art that he liked for the condo. They were oversized pieces, so he was going to drive by tomorrow to pick them up.

After lunch, the four of them had strolled along Commercial Street, bopping in and out of many of the shops. It had been a great afternoon together. Marc and Chris decided to swing by the hardware store before coming back to the condo, leaving Tom and Julie to head home alone.

"Do you want some hot cocoa?" Tom asked.

"Marc has that?"

"No, I brought it in my pack. Remember?"

"I swear that knapsack has magical powers. It's bottomless, like that bag Hermione had in *Harry Potter*."

Tom filled a pan with filtered water from the fridge. He then fired up the front burner to "high" and placed the pan over the flames, making sure he had it perfectly centered on the burner.

"The other gift we could get him is a teakettle for the stove," Tom said. "Or an electronic one like I have. Instead of using this saucepan."

"The gift isn't about you, Tom. I think champagne flutes are the way to go."

"I guess so."

"Flutes would be timeless."

As the water heated, Tom went back to the sectional and

pulled his tablet from his backpack and flipped to his weather app. Julie had managed to get one boot off and was currently fighting with the other one.

"Bad news, Jewels. The blizzard is going to hit soon."

"Really? Shit."

"It looks like the snow will start in the next hour or so. It seems to be picking up speed."

"How bad is the forecast?"

"Maybe a foot by morning. It's sort of hard to tell out here. All that salt air can really dampen it. Turn everything to ice. And the wind is just going to make for some huge drifts."

With one final yank, Julie managed to get her second boot off.

"I'm going upstairs to get my bunny slippers."

Julie walked over to the front door and tossed her boots onto the rug. She grabbed her hat and gloves and bolted upstairs. She still had her jacket on. Tom waited a few minutes for the water to boil and then poured the water for Julie's hot cocoa. He decided he was in the mood for some hot tea and poured himself a cup. As he was filling his mug, the front door opened.

"That was fast," Tom said as Marc and Chris made their way into the kitchen. "How'd you make out?"

"No luck," Marc said. "Their key-making machine was broken."

"Sorry, Marc," Tom replied. "None of us are having any luck today. I couldn't get my candle. You couldn't get your key made."

"But I did find some great artwork. I think it will look nice in here. What's the latest on the storm, Tommy?"

"Snow looks to start within the hour. But it probably won't get bad until after dinner tonight. It's kind of hard to tell. I checked a different weather app on my phone earlier, and it showed the storm moving slower."

Marc paused for several seconds as he stared at the clock on the stove: 3:45 p.m.

"I am going to make a run to Wellfleet," Marc said.

"For a key?" Chris asked. "Can't that wait until tomorrow? Or next time?"

"It's not the key. I want to pick up the hardware for the kitchen cabinets. All the door handles and drawer pulls. It won't take long. Besides, if we're going to be snowed in tomorrow, I can spend the time installing them. It would be great if we can get the key made, but I really want the hardware."

Tom grabbed his tablet and opened his weather app. There was a predictive feature that showed the progress of the path of the storm, including the intensity of the precipitation. You could change the overlays to also show things like temperature and wind. He played around with it for several seconds while Chris and Marc argued about making the run to Wellfleet.

"Marc, can I tag along?" Tom asked.

"Sure, Tommy."

"The snowfall may not get heavy for a few hours. We'll probably just get the light, fluffy stuff first. I was thinking that if we have the time we could stop at a candle store. If there are any near your hardware store."

"It should be about a 20-minute run there and back. Given the roads and snow, figure an hour total, including picking up the hardware. That would give us extra time for you to hit some shops."

"So now we are hauling ass to Wellfleet to get a key, door handles, and that stupid candle?" Chris asked. "I'm exhausted. Just go online to get one, Tom. You practically live online anyway."

"But it has to be local!" Tom yelled back.

"Guys, we don't have time for this," Marc said. "Chris, you don't have to come if you don't want to. Just stay here with Julie."

Tom shoved his tablet back into his backpack and went to get his coat. Chris walked into the kitchen and pulled out the vodka and some club soda and made herself a drink. Julie returned from upstairs wearing her Zombunnies.

"Where are you two going?" Julie asked.

"Wellfleet," Marc replied. "I have to get some stuff for the condo."

"I'm going to see if I can get a candle," Tom said.

"I want to go!" Julie said. "I've never been to Wellfleet! Chris, are you coming, too?"

"Shit," Chris said, taking a sip from her drink before transferring it to a red plastic "to-go" cup. "I don't want to sit here drinking by myself."

"Yay!" Julie said. "Road trip!"

***

Marc gripped the steering wheel tightly. The wind gusts were pushing hard against the Ram. They had just cleared the Provincetown town line and crossed into North Truro on Route 6. Julie smiled as they drove by the tiny Days Cottages. When she and Tom had gone shopping earlier that day she had noticed a lot of paintings of the cottages. All of the paintings had featured sunsets and blue skies.

Snow had already started to fall. Tom's app had been completely wrong on the timing. On this late stormy Saturday afternoon, the normally sunny cheerful cottages looked like they were trapped in a snow globe.

"They are so cute," Julie said.

Tom leaned over to look out Julie's window. He wasn't looking at the cottages. He was focused on the whitecaps on the ocean in the distance behind the cottages. The waves were erratic, angry, and looked like they were coming from all directions. The sky above was a tapestry of silver and dark gray ribbons. Even the normally bright colors of the cottages were completely washed out. He decided to check his weather app again.

"Hey, Marc, this is getting bad," Tom said.

"We're fine, Tommy."

"No, I mean when I look at the weather app, the storm is sort of spinning right toward us."

"I thought you said we had an hour before it would start?" Chris asked. "How bad is it?"

Tom held up his tablet and hit the forecast button to show them the animation of the path of the storm. Chris turned around and took her glasses off so that she could study the map. The storm was massive, spanning over 300 miles across.

The center was currently crossing New Haven, Connecticut. Providence was already getting hit hard, and Boston was just starting to feel the coastal winds and steady snowfall. It was a slow-moving storm, crawling along at roughly 10 mph. Wind gusts were over 60 mph with sustained winds around 45 mph.

"We're totally screwed Marc," Chris said. "We should turn back."

"It's fine, Babe."

"Let me see those glasses, Chris," Julie said.

Chris passed them back to Julie.

"You always look fabulous. I like the red and blue stripes down the side. I've never seen that combo with the tortoise frames before."

"They're Gucci."

Tom glanced at the forecast pattern again.

"It looks like it might spin north, so we may not get hit as bad as everyone else," Tom said. "But you never know. I should check on things back home."

Tom tucked his tablet away and took out his phone. He went to his Recent Calls list, scrolled to "Mom," and selected it. Static crackled through the speaker as he waited for the call to connect.

"Hi, Mom ..."

Julie handed the glasses back to Chris and nodded toward Tom. She mouthed "Mommy" to Chris and grinned. Chris smiled back and took a big gulp from her cup.

"It's fine here," Tom said. "Snow hasn't really started yet. We ... what?"

Tom frowned and let out a loud sigh.

"No, I haven't found a candle yet."

"Oh my God!" Julie exclaimed. "For real? There's a blizzard! Of course, she has to make it about her."

Tom reached over and tried to cover Julie's mouth so she would stop talking. She pushed him away and tapped Chris on the back of her head.

"Give me some of that drink, Becker."

Chris passed the red plastic cup back to Julie.

"OK," Tom said. "Yes ... uh huh ... OK ... yup ..."

Marc had been focused on his driving. He had the Ram in

four-wheel drive, but he could feel the road icing up. The roads were warmer than the air temperature, so the snow was melting and the roads were beginning to ice over. There was a shimmy in the feel of the steering wheel. Marc glanced at his rearview mirror to check on Tom. He could see the stress on his face. He could only imagine the lecture he was getting from his mother.

"OK, sure," Tom said. "Alright ... yes ... OK, look we just got to the store so let me go. Glad you are OK ... yes ... uh huh ... yes ... I know ... yup ..."

Julie snatched Tom's phone from his hands and ended the call.

"Oops," Julie said. "Dropped calls suck."

"Jewels!" Tom protested, although he was secretly relieved that Julie had cut short his mother's complaining about having to hire someone to shovel her driveway because he'd left town.

"You're welcome."

"Can I have my drink back?" Chris asked.

Julie passed the drink back to Chris just as a huge gust of wind jolted the truck, catching Marc off-guard. The truck swerved hard to the left. Chris fumbled with the drink, trying not to spill it. Tom braced himself against the back of Marc's seat. The big Ram seesawed left and right a few times before Marc was able to get it back under control.

"Sorry, guys," Marc said. "That wind came out of nowhere. I may have hit some black ice on the road."

They were out of North Truro and into Truro now. The snowfall had become more intense. It had started to accumulate on the buildings and trees. The road was still clear, but it was becoming slicker as the minutes ticked by. It was 4 p.m.

"I think we should turn around," Julie said.

"Me too," Chris added.

"Tommy?" Marc asked.

Tom looked up at Marc's reflection in the rearview mirror.

"You're the one that needs the cabinet handles for the condo," Tom said.

"The roads are getting bad. I can wait on my stuff. But you

want that candle."

Tom looked out the window. The snow was falling hard. His mother had told him she already had around a foot of snow.

"Let's go back, Marc," Tom urged. "It's not worth it."

"Thank God," Julie said. "Your mom can wait."

Marc drove several hundred more feet before coming upon a small parking lot in front of an old house that had been converted to a store. He pulled into the lot. The dark brown building was lost in the shadows of the large pine trees that surrounded it. This little store was an oddity. Route 6 was known for having dozens of shopping plazas along the Outer Cape to tempt tourists with last-minute gift ideas. They were in small strip malls, three or four storefronts in each building. Most sold t-shirts and souvenirs; a few were restaurants. Truro, however, was mainly residential. There weren't many businesses along the main highway.

A number of big rigs had been traveling behind Marc for the last half-mile, and he was happy to let them pass. Traffic on the eastbound side was heavy with people trying to flee the approaching storm.

As they waited for the road to clear, Tom noticed an old Jeep parked in front of the building. He leaned across Julie to get a better look at it. He pegged it for a late 80s Cherokee. It was most likely a 1989. He had always liked those. This one had several rust spots along the bottom edges of the doors. It was painted red, but it was very faded. Considering how old it was, it was in great shape. That's when he noticed what was behind the Jeep.

"Wait!" Tom yelled.

Marc was just about to pull back onto Route 6.

"What?" Marc asked.

"Look behind the Jeep! Candles!"

The store behind the old Cherokee had the word "Candles" painted across the two front windows.

"Can we run in fast?" Tom asked. "Please?"

"No way," Chris said. "We need to get back to the condo."

Marc glanced at his watch and then into the rearview mirror at Tom.

"OK, Tommy," Marc said. "But let's make this quick."

The building had been there since the 1970s. The roof jutted out to form a covered porch that spanned the front of the building. The plywood roof-sheeting bowed between each of the rafters, creating a warped pattern across the roof. Despite the buckling, the covered patio area provided some much-needed protection from the snow and blistering wind.

Chris and Julie had made it there first, having made a run for it as soon as Marc had turned the engine off.

The wind was merciless. Tom struggled to make his way across the parking lot, instinctively grabbing the back of Marc's coat to keep himself from being blown away or from slipping on the ice. His knapsack was flung over his shoulder. Both men paused briefly and leaned into the wind. The heavy wet snow felt like tiny razor blades as it cut across their skin.

Once the gusts died down, they inched their way forward toward the covered porch where Chris and Julie were waiting for them. Tom peeked inside the passenger's window of the Jeep as he passed by. The interior had seen better days. The entire glovebox was missing. He frowned. He knew he would never let his Ruby get so beat up.

"It's closed," Julie said, pointing at a small faded sign on the inside of the door.

"No!" Tom said. "Shit!"

"Hold on," Chris said.

She pressed her face against one of the big windows, peering through the giant letter "C" in the word "Candles." It was dim inside. No lights were on. But she could see a woman at the back of the store, heading into what looked to be a storage room. Chris walked back to the front door and turned the handle, expecting it to be locked. It wasn't. She continued to turn it counter-clockwise. The latch released.

NINE

The Store

Chris pushed the door open, holding on to it tightly to keep the wind from tearing it from her hands. A small weathered brass bell attached to the doorframe rang, although its sound was muffled by the howling wind.

The store's interior was much larger than its exterior suggested. The attic had been opened up, its floor removed, exposing the building's support beams and giving the space an airy feel. Despite the giant letters sprawled across the front windows, more than candles were sold here. Candles did, however, made up the bulk of the inventory. As with many gift shops on the Cape, the wares for sale comprised a variety of categories, including mugs, key chains, shot glasses and T-shirts. If you could put the name of the town or region on it, this store had it.

Low glass shelves ran across the front windows of the shop and were filled with a variety of candles and candleholders. The wall to the left of the entrance had two small windows from the original attic up along the edge of the ceiling. The rest of it was filled with shelves that ran from the front to the back of the store. They, too, were devoted to candles. Along the back of the store sat another long set of wooden shelves that contained work from local artists, including glassmakers. The center of the store held a variety of displays and clothing racks.

Off to the right sat the checkout counter with the cash register. The glass case beneath the register was filled with cheap jewelry. A back room was carved out into the far-right corner of the building. At one time, the room served as the dining room and bathroom of the house. It was now divided into a stock room, break area, and office.

The store was eerily quiet. No lights were on. The front door whistled as the wind rushed across the frame. A clock hanging over the door hummed loudly, like a wasp protecting its nest.

Sara Johnson emerged from the back room. She was talking on her cell phone and paused as she stared, somewhat shocked, at the four strangers.

Chris looked her up and down and made a quick assessment -- stocky, roughly five-foot-eight, long, wavy, brown hair. She pegged her at over forty years old. *Ancient*, Chris thought. Her face had not a hint of makeup, and her baggy, flannel shirt and faded jeans suggested she cared little about outward appearances.

"I'm going to need to call you back," Sara said. She ended her call and began to walk toward the front of the store. She paused near the main counter to put her cell phone down next to the cash register. "I'm sorry, but we are closed. I need to get home before this storm gets any worse."

Chris walked forward to meet her at the middle of the store. Switching into her realtor business voice, she extended her hand and said, "Chris Becker. Realtor. And you are?"

"Closed," Sara replied.

Chris frowned. That line was usually met with at least a smile.

"Well then, you should have locked the door," Chris said with a smile.

Sara furrowed her brow, disappointed with the young girl's cocky attitude. Marc stepped forward, as he sensed things could quickly go downhill. He knew she was not buying Chris' charm routine.

"Hey, we're sorry," Marc said. "We pulled over to turn

around because of the storm, and we noticed your store. It looked like you were open. My friend here has been candle shopping all day."

Tom inched closer to the woman and smiled. Sara looked him and Marc up and down. Then she turned her gaze over to Julie. Julie pulled her knit hat off, sending her hair into a static mess. Sara managed a slight grin.

"You really shouldn't be out in this weather," Sara said. "There is quite the storm headed our way. Are you local or heading home?"

"We're staying out in Provincetown for the weekend," Chris said. She was determined to win her over. "Have you heard of Seabreeze Village? It's a new townhome complex a few blocks off of Shank Painter."

Sara stared back at Chris, saying nothing.

"No? Well, it's great. We're the first ones to move in. We've got it all to ourselves. It's a really fantastic development."

"Since we're here, do you mind if we take a quick look at your candles?" Marc asked. "Five minutes, ten tops, and then we'll be on our way. I would hate to make this a wasted trip."

"Of course," Sara replied with a smile. "Just so you know, I don't have power so I can't run the register. It would have to be a cash sale."

"I'm fine with that," Tom said.

"Just make it quick," Sara said. "Five minutes."

"Thanks!" Tom said with a big smile.

Tom pulled his knapsack off his shoulder and tossed it on the main counter next to the cash register. The glass-top made a loud cracking sound under the weight of his bag. He quickly pulled it back to make sure there was no damage to the glass. It was fine. He looked over at Sara. She stared back at him with a blank expression on her face. He took the bag off the counter and put it on the floor beside it.

"Sorry," he mumbled.

Tom could see she was upset by the sound the bag made when it hit the glass-top. He tried to lighten the mood.

"I like your Jeep," Tom said. "I have a Wrangler. It's red, too. I've been slowly customizing it. I love it."

There was no reaction from his fellow Jeep owner.

"Those old Cherokees are classics," Tom continued. "I had wanted to drive my Ruby out but couldn't take her this trip. Next time. I would love to pop the doors off and drive along the ocean through the sand dunes. How long have you had yours? Did you ever do any customizations to it?"

"I don't know," Sara replied. "It was my dad's. He's dead now."

"Oh," Tom said.

"Are you looking for anything particular?" Sara asked. "I have some new ones. They just came in."

"I'm kind of picky," Tom replied as he walked away. "I really prefer to look around by myself. I'll know it when I see it."

Chris, Tom, and Marc quickly spread out to different parts of the store. Julie walked over to the main counter. There was a stand with sunglasses on it. As Julie adjusted her hair in the mirror, she noticed a tortoise-framed pair of glasses with red and blue stripes. They were cheap knockoffs of the Gucci ones that Chris wore. She smirked and briefly considered getting them. That's when she noticed the stack of three books next to the cash register. She picked the top one up to confirm her suspicion. It was indeed the same urban legend book she had brought along on the trip.

"Excuse me," Julie said, as she looked over at Sara.

Sara came walking over to Julie and raised her eyebrows.

"Are you familiar with this book?" Julie asked. She held up the copy that was lying on the counter.

"Yes. Yes, I am."

"You own a candle store. One of the legends is about people being killed and made into candles. It supposedly happened in Wellfleet. Are you familiar with it?"

Sara laughed. Chris was at the far end of the store opposite the main counter. She turned around, surprised to hear the woman laughing. Chris smiled. She was glad to see Julie was able to lighten the mood and turned to walk back to join them.

"Those stories are all silly," Sara said. "I can't tell you how many people read these things and think they're all true. And they aren't. Well, most anyway."

"Most?" Julie asked.

100

"These legends all start because of one event that happened a long time ago. The story gets passed from person to person, and over time, it changes until it's nothing like what really happened. Sometimes multiple stories get combined into one. Then someone throws it in a book, and everyone thinks it's real."

"I see."

Chris was now standing next to Julie.

"So, the candlestick-killer thing in the book?" Chris asked. "None of that is true?"

"Is that the one about wicks for bones?" Sara asked.

"Yes," Julie said.

"My point exactly," Sara replied. "Bones don't burn like wicks."

"That's what I said!" Chris replied with a laugh.

Julie looked around the store for Tom. He was going through the candles along the front window. "Tom, any luck?"

"Not yet," Tom answered.

"Try looking back over where I was," Chris said. "There are a bunch of candles along the side shelves."

Tom ignored Chris and continued to go through the shelves at the front of the store. Julie put the book back down onto the glass top. Sara turned and walked around behind the main counter. Her right leg ached, so she took a seat on a small stool.

"Chris, you know what we need?" Julie asked. "A new candle for the table on the back patio. That handle is broken. For the key."

"What key?" Chris asked, smiling.

"Oh my God ... don't start!" Turning to Sara, Julie asked, "Do you have any big metal outdoor candles? For bugs?"

"Bugs?" Sara asked.

"Citronella ones," Chris added.

"I don't really know," Sara said.

"C'mon, Julie," Chris said with a laugh. She took Julie by the elbow and turned toward the back corner of the store. "Now tell me where the fucking key is!"

"The key is under the fucking candle! Don't get me going, Becker. Just drop it!"

Sara frowned as the two walked away laughing. She was growing impatient.

Marc was at the back of the store next to the entrance to the stock room. A plastic sign that read "Employees Only" was pinned to the top of the door frame. To the left was a shelving unit with a large assortment of knick-knacks, including some glass plates. They looked handmade. There were also some beautiful hand-carved wooden bowls. But the glass plates had caught his eye. There were three, all the same size, but different colors. One was a deep red, another lime green, and the other, a vibrant blue. Each was the same design and less than a foot in diameter. He looked around and saw Chris and Julie in the corner at a giant wall of candles. They were still laughing.

"Hey, Tommy," Marc called out.

Tom stopped what he was doing and walked back to see Marc.

"What do you think of these glass plates?" Marc asked. "For in the kitchen. Just to put out on the counter up against the backsplash."

"I like them. Will they go with the artwork you're getting?"

"Totally. I decided not to go with a single color. I'm doing primary colors instead."

"Sounds perfect."

"Smile!" Julie yelled from across the store.

Tom and Marc turned to look. She had her phone up to take their picture. Marc pulled Tom back up against him with both arms and rested his chin on the top of Tom's head. Julie snapped a few pictures. After a quick glance at the results, she gave them a thumbs up. Marc turned back to look at the shelving to see if there was anything he might have missed.

"Hey, check this out," Marc said. He reached around the side of the shelving unit to retrieve an archery arrow. The broadhead tip was a silver 3-blade fixed design. Each blade had a unique kidney-shaped opening cut into it. The shaft was black, and the fletchings were bright yellow. Marc took a few steps back and held his arm outstretched, balancing the arrow flat across his hand. It was impressively lightweight. He wondered if it was carbon fiber. "We can try this, too, when we get back home."

"Try what?"

"Archery."

"You know archery?" Tom shook his head. *Is there anything this guy can't do?*

"There is a great practice range up in Lincoln out in the woods. I have gone a few times. It teaches you great hand-eye coordination. It's a total confidence-builder. Which, to be honest, is something you could use."

"OK."

"Don't 'yes' me like you did with kickboxing. I'm serious, Tommy. No excuses."

"OK, Marc, I promise to take it up once we're back home."

Sara looked on as the four strangers roamed throughout the store. She was getting annoyed. They seemed to be looking at everything but candles. None of them had stopped to see the display she had set up earlier.

"Are you almost done?" Sara called out from behind the store counter. "Your five minutes are up."

Tom walked back to the store counter. Marc continued to study the arrow for a bit before finally tucking it back along the side of the shelf.

"Maybe you can help me," Tom said to Sara. "I'm looking for a candle for my mom. She wants something with a beach scent made locally. Blue or tan. Something unique."

Sara looked at the battery-operated clock on the wall over the front door. The buzz and hum from the spinning minute hand were getting on her nerves. It was almost 4:30 p.m.

"Follow me," Sara said. She stood up and ran her hand across her leg. The wound throbbed tenderly beneath her clothing.

Sara took Tom to a small table set up in the middle of the store. The table was only about three feet in height and the same in diameter. The shape reminded Tom of the outdoor patio table back at the condo. But instead of it being made of iron and mosaic tile, this one was made of wood, possibly cherry. Or at least it was stained to look like cherry. It appeared to have inlaid nickel and turquoise at the bottom of the feet, which extended up a few inches. There were about a dozen candles on the table, stacked in a circle to form a round pyramid.

"These are all made here on the Cape," Sara said. "If you pop one open, you'll notice the wick is a flat piece of wood."

Tom picked up the candle from the top of the display. It was a square glass jar with rounded edges, roughly four inches by four inches. It had a glass lid with a metal hinge that wrapped around a circular neck on top. The lid had a thick rubber seal with a hinged lock. He liked that the wax inside was tan. The sticker on the back looked like it came from an inkjet printer and simply read: "FlickerWood Candles." He frowned after reading the small sticker on the top of the lid -- "Sesame." He popped the lid open and inhaled. It did indeed smell like sesame. All the candles were the same light tan color, but they were all marked either "Sesame" or "Ginger."

"Do you have any other scents?" Tom asked.

"Sorry, that's all I have. They were just made."

Sara could see the disappointment on Tom's face.

"It might not smell like the beach, but it's all local ingredients like you said," Sara said, hoping to convince him to buy it.

Julie and Chris were only about twenty feet away at a large wall of candles. Julie walked over to the small table with Tom and Sara. She grabbed the candle from Tom and took a whiff.

"Sesame!" Julie proclaimed. "That smells wonderful. Asian. I love Asian food. This is making me hungry. We should do Thai tomorrow."

Julie took a few moments to inspect the candle design.

"Tom, you should get this," Julie continued. "I love this jar design with the flip-top lid. And what's that wick inside? I've never seen a flat wick. It looks like it came off of a clarinet."

Tom stared at Julie and raised his right eyebrow.

"What?" Julie asked. "I told you my parents made me take music class in high school. Don't judge!"

"The wood wicks are all hand-carved," Sara said. "They don't burn like a normal wick. They crackle and flicker."

"And that's wood, not bone?" Julie asked with a smile.

Sara laughed and turned to Tom and asked, "So what do you think?"

"I'm not sure."

"I give up," Julie said. She handed the candle back to Tom.

Julie spun around and worked her way back over to Chris who was busy going through several shelves of candles along the side wall in the back of the store.

"Chris, he is impossible," Julie said. "Are you having any luck here?"

"Not really," Chris replied. "There are lots of brown and blue candles on this wall. But I don't know if they are local or not. And I don't really smell anything."

"At this point, I don't care. Just get something that smells like the ocean, and we can blow this clam shack."

"There's an idea. A clam-scented candle."

"That's gross."

"Beach at low tide? Crusty barnacles? Fisherman needing a bath?"

"Oh my God ... stop!" Julie began to laugh. She opened a few more candles and inhaled. "Nothing! Is my nose broken?"

"Dead seagull? That would smell nice in his mom's bathroom."

Chris was now giggling.

"Stop it, Becker!"

"I can't smell anything either, Julie."

Chris turned to face Tom and Sara in the middle of the store.

"Excuse me?" Chris called out. "Hello? Lady? Mrs. Closed? Are any of these scented?"

Sara turned her attention from Tom and looked over at Chris and frowned. She pointed up toward the ceiling against the wall that Chris and Julie were at. In unison, both turned and looked up to see a four-foot wide sign hanging from the beam above the candle display they were standing in front of. It read:

UNSCENTED

Julie's jaw dropped. She and Chris looked at each other and burst out laughing. The snorts and deep breaths from Julie came out at an extremely rapid pace. Chris bent over and put her hands on Julie's shoulders as she laughed out loud.

"Oh my God!" Julie screamed.

"How long have we been sniffing these fucking things?" Chris said through her laughter.

Marc finished looking at the glass plates and decided it was best to just leave. They had overstayed their welcome, especially with Chris and Julie swearing and laughing up a storm. He walked over to Tom and Sara in the middle of the store. Sara was glaring at Chris and Julie.

"What's the scoop, Tommy? Are we good?"

"I like everything except the scent. It's a cool candle. They make it here, and I have never seen a wick like that. But it doesn't smell like the beach."

"Does it have to be perfect? If you like everything else about it, why not get it? What if … what if … Look, buy this now. We have tomorrow to look around. We can even stop at some stores on the drive home if you change your mind."

"True."

Tom glanced back down at the stack of candles. Marc was right. He was totally overthinking this. There were a few more weeks before Christmas, so he had plenty of time later to get something else if necessary.

"I'll take it," Tom said to Sara.

"Follow me," Sara said. She was relieved this was finally over. "It's going to be twenty."

Tom and Sara walked over to the main counter at the side of the store. She walked behind it and pulled out a brown paper bag and put the candle in it. Tom handed her a twenty-dollar bill and took the bag.

"Guys, let's fly!" Marc called out from the front door.

"Oh, that gives me another scented-candle idea," Chris said to Julie, grabbing her by the shoulders and looking her dead in the eye. "Flies on Fries! A classic beach scent!"

"Stop already!" Julie howled. Tears were running down her face. She shoved Chris away from her. Chris laughed and took a few steps back. As Chris turned toward the door, she slammed straight into the wooden display table stacked with the FlickerWood Candles. She tried to catch herself, but it was too late. Her left leg smashed into the bottom support beam of the table, kicking it sideways. All the candles slid off. She lunged forward but only made it worse, sending some of them flying several feet through the air.

"Oh my God!" Julie yelled.

"Shit!" Chris said.

The sound of shattering glass jars echoed throughout the store. Marc and Tom spun around to see what the commotion was all about. The cherry table survived the fall, but the candles did not fare so well. Sara remained motionless, staring in disbelief from behind the counter.

"Do you have any idea what you've done?" Sara yelled. Her tone had shifted dramatically. She was no longer politely annoyed and tolerant of them being in the store. This was full-blown anger. Rage. "Those candles were just made this week! That was our entire batch!"

Tom, Chris, Julie, and Marc stood speechless. Julie bent down and started to collect the candle jars and fragments. Marc walked toward the counter and reached into his pocket and pulled out his wallet.

"Let me pay for these," Marc said. "Really. How much do you ..."

"Leave," Sara said sternly.

"No, please, I insist."

"Leave! Leave! Leave!" Sara screamed, her voice doubling in volume with each spoken word. She clenched her hands into two fists and repeatedly pounded on the glass countertop.

Marc stopped his approach to the counter. He slowly slid his wallet back into his pocket. The anger and hate being projected at him made him very uneasy.

"Do you have any idea what we went through to make these candles?" Sara asked. "Do you know the cost?"

"I told you we would pay," Marc said calmly.

"Oh, you will pay!" Sara said defiantly. "All of you will pay!"

Sara slammed her fists down one last time. The glass countertop immediately shattered into several large pieces.

The sound was deafening.

Nobody moved.

Sara slowly raised her arms up and checked her quivering hands. The glass had splintered into several different-sized shards. Miraculously, none of them had cut her hands open. She unclenched her fists and walked around the counter to the middle of the store where the FlickerWood Candle display used to be. Julie let go of the chunks of candles she had been collecting and left them on the floor. She slowly stood up.

"Get out. Now!" Sara insisted. Her voice trembled with anger. "Now!"

Sara turned her gaze from Tom, to Marc, to Chris, and to Julie. Sara then grabbed Julie and shoved her into Chris.

"Do you intend to break the rest of them?" Sara screamed. "You have ruined endless days of hard work! I said leave!"

The light in the store was very dim now. The sun was close to setting, and the dark cloudy skies had killed what little light remained. Marc turned the handle on the front door. The wind from outside blasted it open, sending huge wet snowflakes inside. The bell above the door chimed. Shards of glass from the candle jars rattled as the wind blew them across the floor. Sara knelt to inspect the damage.

Chris and Julie quickly made their way toward the door, trying their best not to step on the broken glass. Tom had a deer in the headlights look about him as he clutched his brown shopping bag. Marc grabbed him by the shoulders and pushed him to the door.

Tom stopped and turned for one final look at the disaster they were leaving in their wake. Sara was on her hands and knees, staring at the pile of broken candles, slowly trying to sort through the remnants.

"I'm sorry," Tom said.

Sara stopped what she was doing and looked up at the four strangers standing in the doorway. She was disgusted by their behavior. She was filled with anger and hate.

"There is a price to be paid for your disrespect," Sara said solemnly.

Marc pushed the other three through the doorway and quickly slammed it closed. He motioned everyone toward the truck. By now, it was covered in a thin layer of snow. Marc did not bother to clear the windows. All four quickly jumped in. Marc put the wipers on high, turned the defroster to maximum, and made a U-turn to take them back to

Provincetown.

Sara stood up and looked out the window as the giant silver Ram tore out of the parking lot heading back down Route 6. She turned to the cherry table that was lying sideways on the floor. She set it upright and wiggled it. It seemed solid. She held her hands out and quietly inspected them. They were still trembling slightly. She took a deep breath to calm herself.

She looked down at the floor. There had been a dozen candles on the table. She sold one. All but four of the eleven remaining candles were completely shattered, and of those four, two were cracked.

"Twenty bucks for ten candles," Sara said out loud, speaking to nothing but an empty room. "What a waste. I knew I should have made those kids leave."

Sara looked at the clock on the wall. It was getting late, and darkness was setting in.

"Another mess to clean up," Sara said, resigned to the reality of the situation. "Now ... where would I find a dustpan and brush?"

Sara looked around the store and behind the counter. Then it dawned on her to check the back room. That was when her cell phone rang. She walked over to the main counter to get her phone. Luckily it had been on the side that had not broken.

"Hello, Mother."

She paused and listened.

"Yes, I know I said I would call you back. I got ... delayed."

Sara paused to listen for several more seconds.

"Don't get upset, but we had a bit of a problem here at the store."

Another pause.

"Are you sitting down? Because you aren't going to like what I have to say. These kids came into the store. They ... there was an accident."

Sara sighed as she briefly tolerated the lecture coming through the phone.

"Listen," Sara interrupted. "Listen! So, these rich kids from Provincetown came in. There were a couple of real wise-asses in the group. There was an accident with our display ... but ..."

Another pause as a series of questions came through.

"One of them knocked over the table with our candles on them."

Sara pulled the phone back from her ear as the yelling escalated. She waited patiently for things to calm down.

"Two."

Again, she had to pull the phone away.

"Yes, only two. I'll take care of it ... no, I'll ... trust me ... I know I screwed up."

Sara listened as a series of instructions came through the earpiece.

"Yes, I know that in times like these ... No, I do. I do. It will be OK. Trust me."

Sara paused a bit more until she was sure her mother had finally started to calm down.

"I am leaving soon. I just need to clean things up here. I'll be home before you know it. We'll figure things out then."

Sara listened patiently one last time, nodding in agreement with the suggestions her mother was making. She was much calmer now, especially since she knew what she had to do.

"Don't worry, I'll fix it. All of it. They will pay. They will all pay. Goodbye, Mother."

Sara ended the call and slid the phone into her pocket. She limped back to the counter and smiled when she reached the corner. There, against the side of the display, was Tom's backpack.

TEN

Lost and Found

Marc opened the front door to the townhouse and slid his hand along the wall, searching for the light switches. The porch light came on with the flip of the switch and spilled across the hood of the big Ram truck. It was the only vehicle in the desolate complex.

Marc stepped into the hallway and ran his fingers over three touch sensitive dimmer switches. After a brief pause, the kitchen, living room, and dining room lights all slowly rose to their preset levels. He glanced at the clock on the stove in the kitchen. It was a few minutes before 5 p.m.

Julie pushed past Marc and collapsed onto the hallway floor in front of him, the caked snow on her boots melting onto the small hallway carpet.

"Oh my God, I am so glad to be home," she said as she struggled to free her foot from her right boot. "That lady was fucking whacked. Seriously. Scared the shit out of me. I still can't believe how she shoved me."

Marc walked over to the dining room table and sat down to remove his construction boots. The bottoms were packed with snow and mud. He glanced around the path from the front door to the other rooms and realized he was going to need a much bigger and more heavy-duty rug to catch the dirt and grime that was getting tracked in.

"She just shattered that counter," Tom said. He walked over to the kitchen and slid the brown bag with the candle onto the island.

Chris tossed her leather jacket onto the coat rack on the wall next to the bathroom and kicked her boots off, leaving them right next to Julie, who was still sitting on the floor fighting to get her boot off.

"Your mother better like that candle, Tom," Chris said.

"Are we doing this again?" Tom asked. "Why are you mad at me? You're the one that knocked the display over!"

"It was an accident!"

Tom walked over to Julie and placed his hand on top of her head to steady himself as he reached down to untie his boots. He then hung his coat neatly on the rack.

"Are you OK, Tommy?" Marc asked.

Marc had been very concerned on the drive home. Tom seemed quite rattled in the back of the truck. Initially, he and Chris had yelled at each other for about five minutes. Once Marc had managed to calm them down, Tom's only words the rest of drive back were: "She shattered that counter."

"I'm fine, Marc," Tom replied. "I just ... I've never seen so much rage before."

Chris headed into the kitchen and started pulling bottles and mixers out to make martinis. She just wanted to forget everything that had happened. Not only the events at the store, but also the fight with Tom on the ride home, as well as Marc once again playing peacemaker and trying to make things right by siding with Tom.

Chris looked over at Julie in the hallway and asked, "Cocktail?"

Julie was still sitting on the floor. She let out a groan as she finally yanked her right boot off and sent it flying into the kitchen island. She immediately turned her attention to the left one.

"Only if it's scented!" Julie replied in a deadpan tone.

Chris burst out laughing. Julie started to giggle.

"Seriously, guys?" Marc asked. His voice was deeper than usual, and very stern. "The least you can do is show some class. You were both completely disrespectful. She didn't even want us in that store. It was closed. She was kind enough to let us shop for a bit. All you two did was laugh and swear half the time and then, Chris, you go and knock that table over and break everything that was on it."

"Disrespectful ..." Julie said quietly.

"You offered to pay for it," Chris said.

"Right," Marc countered. "*I* offered. *Me.* I didn't see you reach for your money."

Julie finally got her second boot removed. She stood up and pulled her hat off, sending her hair into a static frenzy. The rug in the front hallway was now soaked, forcing Julie to walk across it on tiptoes to avoid getting her socks wet.

"Something was wrong with her," Julie said.

She collapsed on the sectional, pulled her socks off, and curled her bare feet under her legs.

"I mean like mentally wrong," Julie continued. "She wasn't all there. And that limp of hers bothered me. Worst of all, her comment about making us pay? Guys, that is straight out of the Wellfleet candle legend in that book. I've read that story a few times. Trust me."

"Enough with that stupid legend," Chris said.

"No way," Julie said. "There are too many similarities."

"Enough!" Marc said. "Both of you. I was really disappointed with you guys. Not you, Tommy."

Chris glared at Marc. She rattled the cocktail shaker vigorously. Julie looked over, and Chris just shook her head in disappointment. Then she raised her right eyebrow and nodded ever so slightly toward Tom. Julie nodded back. Marc was supporting Tom, not Chris. Julie knew that Chris had to be seething on the inside.

"Look, we're all home now," Julie said. "Who knows how long this storm is going to last. So let's enjoy some drinks, have some food, and relax. OK? It could be a long night. What's the latest forecast, Tom?"

Tom started to pull his phone from his pocket but decided he would rather pull it up on his tablet. The larger screen would make it easier to see the full weather map. He looked for his bag but then remembered he had taken it with him when they left for Wellfleet earlier. Then it dawned on him.

"Oh my God," Tom said.

"You sound like Julie," Chris said with a laugh.

"My pack. My backpack!"

"What?" Marc asked. He could see the color draining from Tom's face.

Marc stood up from the dining room table and carried his boots over to the rug in the hallway.

"I left it back at the store. It's at the store!"

"Well, it was getting a bit beat up anyway, wasn't it?" Chris asked. "Time for a new one if you ask me."

"No. No. You don't understand. Everything is in there."

Tom started to shake as the reality of what had happened began to set in. His cheeks went from pale to flush.

"My tablet. My cords. My battery backup. Even the keys to my house! It's all there! All of it!"

"Why the hell do you have your keys in there?" Chris asked.

"Because I do! I keep everything important in it!"

Marc walked over and put his arm around Tom to try and steady him. Tom felt his eyes begin to well up with tears. That pack contained everything important to him. He had to get it back. He turned and looked up at Marc.

"Marc?" Tom pleaded. He didn't know what to ask for, only that Marc would fix it. Marc fixed everything.

Marc stared down at Tom and looked into his blue-gray eyes as they started to fill with tears. He could see how distraught he was. Julie was silent. She understood how important that backpack was to Tom. Chris was fully engrossed in her martini.

It was just after 5 p.m. and the snow was falling steadily.

"OK," Marc finally said. "OK, look. This is what we're going to do. Tom, you and Julie are going to stay here while Chris and I go back to the store to get your pack."

"What?" Chris yelled. She poured a bit more booze into her martini glass. "I'm not going anywhere."

"Yes, you are," Marc replied in a slow and steady voice, annunciating each word.

"Why me?"

"Because out of the four of us you are the one that needs to apologize. You know who was the only one of us to say 'sorry' back there? Tommy. I heard him on the way out. You broke all of those candles and simply left. I'm not going back there to clean up the mess you made. You are."

"How do we even know if she's still there?" Chris asked. She was desperately trying to think of a way out of this. "I'm sure she is long gone by now."

"Can we call the store?" Julie asked.

"Does anyone even know the name of it?" Marc asked. There was a moment of silence. "Tommy, the candle bag."

Tom grabbed the wrinkled brown paper bag and turned it around several times. His hands were trembling. He removed the candle and smoothed the bag out and held it under the light, turning it over and over.

"It's plain," Tom said. "No name or number."

"I think it was called Unusually Unscented Candles," Chris said with a laugh. Julie did not laugh along this time. Tom was on the verge of a complete meltdown. She stayed in the living room, letting the other three battle this out in the kitchen.

"Maybe I can find it online," Julie said. She pulled her phone out and waited for the browser to load.

"Jewels, wait!" Tom said. He pulled his phone out and unlocked it and swiped a few times. "I can find my tablet. I have it on an app. Both the phone and the tablet. All my electronics. I can track them."

Julie jumped off the sectional and ran over to the kitchen island. She, Tom, and Marc were on one side. Chris was on the other. Tom was still visibly shaking. Marc put both hands on his shoulders and gave him a light squeeze.

"Relax, Tommy."

The shaking stopped.

Marc and Julie watched as Tom tapped through his phone. A map came up and slowly panned across the Outer Cape. It finally settled on Route 6, right in the middle of Truro. Tom looked up at Marc and smiled.

"Tommy, you are a genius. That's the store. That's right where we were when we turned off to head back. I'm sure of it."

"Really?" Tom asked.

"I've been driving back and forth for months. I practically have it memorized. Your pack is totally there."

"But what if ... what's her name? What *was* her name?"

"Closed. Her name was Closed," Chris said. "Seriously. She never told us." Chris was now sulking on the other side of the island watching the other three go through Tom's phone.

"What if she's not there?" Tom asked.

"We take a chance," Marc said. "Worst case scenario, if we get there and she's not, we can call the cops and see if they can open it up or track the owner down. But chances are she's still there. She had a big mess to clean up."

Chris and Marc locked eyes over his last comment.

"I don't think you should go," Julie said.

"Thanks," Chris said.

"No, I mean either of you. Nobody should go back to that store."

"I can deal with the weather, Julie," Marc said. "It's really not that far away."

"Not that," Julie said. "It's the legend!"

"Not this again," Chris said with a sigh.

Julie walked back to the sectional and sat in the corner, facing the kitchen. Her book was on the coffee table. She grabbed it and flipped to the story from Wellfleet. She turned a few pages to find the section that concerned her.

"Listen!" Julie said. "In the book, it says that the victims were always people that they felt disrespected them. They made them pay for their contempt with their lives. That is exactly what that crazy woman was yelling at us when we ran out the door! I can read it to you!"

Marc, Tom, and Chris took turns looking at one another and then at Julie. Chris finally let out a laugh.

"You're being a bit emotional," Chris said.

"The fuck I am!" Julie yelled.

"This isn't helping, Julie," Marc said. "We are wasting time here. Chris and I are going back to the store. Right now. End of discussion."

Julie flung her book down by her side and folded her arms

in anger.

"Let me come with you," Tom said.

"No, Tommy. You are rattled enough. Chris and I will handle this."

"But ..." Chris started to complain.

"Christine, please," Marc said. "This is important."

"Fine," Chris said. She turned and grabbed a red plastic cup from the stack on the back counter and poured the rest of her martini into it. She then topped it off with what was left in the shaker. "Let's go."

"Wait," Tom said. "Before you go. Hold on."

Tom flipped through his phone a few times and tapped for several seconds. He turned back to Marc.

"OK, I turned off my security so the phone won't lock you out. The app is open so you can track the tablet. Take my phone and use it to find it."

"Tommy, I know where the store is."

"But what if she finds the bag and decides to take it?"

"I seriously doubt that's going to happen."

"Please, Marc, I would feel a lot better if you did. My world is in that backpack."

"OK, Tommy. If you insist."

Marc took the phone from Tom and handed it to Chris. She rolled her eyes, annoyed that she was being forced to go looking for a lost backpack during a blizzard. She knew she probably owed it to Tom, but she wasn't about to admit it.

"Do I need to know anything about this tracking app?" Chris asked Tom.

"Not really. It's just like a map. I set it to find the tablet. You can also use it to find my laptop and even my mom's phone. So don't jump back to that list. Just follow the dot on the map."

"OK, got it."

"Thanks for doing this, Chris."

"Sure."

Tom and Chris briefly smiled at one another.

"OK, guys, this shouldn't take us long," Marc said. "If the roads cooperate and she is still at that store we'll be back in under an hour. Chris or I will call you once we have it. Maybe you two can have dinner ready for when we get back?"

"You bet," Tom said. "Leftovers will be warm and ready for you!"

Marc walked back over to the dining room table with his construction boots and proceeded to lace them back up. Chris headed to the hallway and slipped her boots and coat back on. She double-checked to make sure she had her glasses and then grabbed her drink off the counter. Marc quickly joined her and flicked off the hallway light.

"Be back soon, Tommy," Marc said.

Tom threw his arms around Marc and hugged him tightly. "Thank you, Marc."

"Don't worry, everything is going to be fine. I promise."

Marc kissed Tom on the top of his head, turned and opened the door. Chris immediately exited onto the front porch. The wind was stronger than earlier. Snow blasted deep into the front hallway.

"Marc," Julie called out from the living room.

"Yes?" Marc asked. His coat flapped from the wind blowing behind him.

"Watch your back," Julie said. "And make it fast. I don't trust that woman. In the legend ..."

"I'll watch my back," Marc said. "But I need you to stop reading those urban legends. See both of you soon."

ELEVEN

Truro

The big Ram struggled to make its way up the driveway. Luckily the crushed stone helped with the traction. Marc slowly eased the truck over the crest and onto the road and turned right. The street was covered in snow. The only tracks were the ones on the opposite side from their recent return. He began the slow crawl to make his way back to Route 6.

Chris sat silently in the passenger's seat, her red cup in one hand and Tom's cell phone in the other. The wind howled as it blew past the truck's side mirrors. Mother Nature was doing her best to turn them back around.

"What are you thinking?" Marc finally asked.

"The map shows his tablet is still at the store," Chris responded.

"Not about that app, Chris. What are *you* thinking? I know you're mad at me. Talk to me."

Chris took a sip of her drink. It was warm, which she found surprising given how cold it was outside. Normally, she would find the mild burn of the alcohol calming. But now, sitting in this big truck that she hated, driving through a storm that worried her, she didn't find it the least bit satisfying.

"What am I thinking?" She paused to collect her thoughts. There were so many of them swirling around in her head. "I'm thinking ... Marc ..."

"Talk to me, Babe."

Chris placed her drink in the cup holder and rested Tom's phone on her lap. She took her glasses off and wiped the lenses with her sweater. She glanced at Tom's phone to make sure they were still on track.

"I feel ... I feel a lot of different things. I get that I screwed up at the store, OK? As much as I hate getting dragged out in this storm, you're right. I was a total ass. I need to own up to that. I pride myself on building great relationships with my clients. And even though that old lady wasn't a client, she didn't deserve that."

"I'm glad you understand."

"But that's not what's bothering me."

Marc gripped the leather-wrapped wheel a little tighter as the wind gusts picked up. He felt the big truck slide sideways a bit.

"It has to do with you, me, and Tom," Chris continued. "I feel like you are always taking his side. You never back me. Why do you always support him and not me?"

Marc looked over at Chris. He expected to see her staring down into her cup or gazing out the window. Instead, Chris was looking directly at him. She looked angry. Marc smiled.

"Are you jealous?" Marc asked. "Because if you are, that is totally adorable." Marc started to chuckle.

"I kind of am!" Chris said. "Seriously!"

"I'm sorry," Marc replied. He regained his composure and turned his attention back to the task of driving. They were almost to the main highway.

"Look, Babe, I love you. You know that. I'm sorry if you feel that I side with Tommy all the time. Maybe I do. But when I look at Tommy, I see someone that needs propping up. The guy just lacks confidence. He comes across as bossy, and Mr. Know It All, but deep down I think he's very insecure. You're the opposite. You have confidence in spades."

Marc slowed as they approached the turn onto Route 6. He allowed the truck to drift through the corner. The highway was completely empty. As he pressed the gas pedal, he could feel all four tires struggle to gain traction. The shimmy in the steering wheel was a bit stronger than it had been earlier, but the snow was falling at roughly the same pace. The headlights illuminated a wall of snowflakes as they rushed past the truck. He had the defroster set on high to help keep the windows from icing up.

"Look, Marc, after we were dating for a couple of weeks, you told me more about your past. That ... well ..."

"I've dated guys before?"

"Yes."

"I told you, Babe. I don't see gender."

"I know."

"Are you worried that maybe that somehow means I don't love you or something?

"No, Marc. I know that you love me. I do."

"Good."

"But the way you defend Tom sometimes. I just feel kind of ... well, kind of threatened."

"I'm all yours, Babe. Never doubt that. You keep dumping me. Almost monthly, lately. How many times do I keep running back to you? Every time."

Marc reached over and squeezed her hand. Chris held it gently.

"Then why are you always pushing me?" Chris asked. "You never push back on him. Only me."

Marc briefly took his eyes off the road to look at Chris. She was gazing out the side window again, retreating.

"You know, you and Tommy are a lot alike. You are the biggest clams, always keeping your feelings inside. You can be cold at times, Chris. I know you are protecting yourself. I wish you would let me in more."

Chris continued to look out the window. They were passing by the sand dunes near the Provincetown town line. She didn't like being compared to Tom.

"I look at Tommy, and I see someone who is broken. I look at you, and I see someone that needs guidance. That's the difference. That's why I'm always pushing you to take the high road and not start some pissing match with him. I want you to set the example. It gets tiring. I feel like I always have to referee the fights between you and Tommy. And even now, this mess with the broken candles. You made no effort to fix things while we were there."

"But that woman freaked out!"

"I know she did, Chris. My point is that once again I'm the one making you do the right thing. To fix a mess that you created. I wish you would just try to work *with* me instead of against me. You are so good at your job. So professional. But then you pull this stupid shit that I have to go and fix."

Chris downed a big chug of her drink, swallowed, and took a deep breath. She felt the hint of a buzz coming on.

"You know, Julie and I had a long talk yesterday while you two were at the grocery store," Chris said. "She told me a lot about Tom. His mom. His dad. I actually kind of feel bad for him. He sounds like he's had it rough."

"He has," Marc said. "His mom is a real piece of work. Did I ever tell you how much she used to stop over to inspect my kitchen renovations at his condo?"

"No."

"It was like, weekly. And often completely unannounced. Sometimes she would show up when Tommy wasn't even there. She would point out what she thought were mistakes and ask me if I would be correcting them. She also didn't like the white cabinets. At all. Thought they should be cream-colored.

"Poor Tommy kept second-guessing all of his choices because she would keep telling him they were all wrong. I eventually had to tell him I would have to start charging him to go back and change things. Or that it was too late. Like custom-painting the cabinets cream. I could have totally done that. But it would have looked like shit with the rest of the design. So, I told him that the finish I had done in white would not allow me to paint over it without completely stripping it all down and possibly ruining the wood. It was a complete lie, but I didn't know how else to get him to take my side instead of his mom's.

"He and his mom had this big argument about it right in front of me. It was bizarre to watch, but also kind of sad. That was the moment when I realized how damaged Tommy was."

Marc paused.

"Maybe damaged is too strong of a word," he continued. "It just made me understand why Tommy is ... well, Tommy. If that makes sense."

Chris thought about her own dad and how he tried so hard to force her into the family business. She tried to imagine if her dad tried to inflict that much control over everything else that she tried to do. Like Tom's mom did.

"I get it, Marc."

Tom's phone flashed a message notification. It was from Julie.

Any luck?!?!

Chris typed a quick reply.

Still driving. Roads are bad.

"I know you and your dad have issues, Chris. You refuse to open up about them. But I have to believe they're nowhere near as bad as what Tommy has gone through. You can tell me anything. I'm here for you."

Chris looked over at Marc and smiled. Marc gave her a quick glance and grinned back. He leaned over, and aimed his cheek in her direction. She propped herself up on the huge center console and gave him a gentle kiss on the corner of his lips.

"Trust me, Babe. You don't need to be jealous. You have my heart."

"Thanks, Marc."

"You just need to stop being such a brat all of the time."

Chris adjusted her hair, turned back to Marc, and stuck her tongue out.

"Brat!" Marc teased. "So how are we doing with the map? Visibility sucks, but we should be at the store soon."

Chris was glad they had talked, but she still had bigger concerns about the future of their relationship. She tapped the Refresh button on Tom's phone.

"Shit!" she exclaimed. "The tablet. It's not at the store anymore. It's moving away from us."

"Away?"

"Yes. It looks like ... yes ... I think it's ... it's moving toward ... Wellfleet."

Marc shook his head. This was not turning out to be the easy trip he had hoped for.

***

Marc slowed to 20 mph as they crossed into Wellfleet. The crosswinds had become very heavy. Route 6 was desolate. They had passed one snowplow heading east about five miles back, but that was it.

"It's moved way out toward the ocean," Chris said. "You're going to want to take a left. I'll let you know which one."

Another message notification from Julie appeared.

> What is taking so long? Please respond
> with an update. (This is Tom.)

Chris swiped it away without replying. She had to stay focused on the map. The blinking dot indicating the location of the tablet had finally stopped moving. It would only be a few more minutes for them to reach it.

"OK, it's coming up soon," Chris said. She alternated her gaze from the map to the windshield as she watched for the turn. "There. That's it."

Marc let his truck slowly coast down to a crawl as he approached the turn, concerned he might hit a patch of black ice. After the turn, he looked to Chris for guidance.

"OK, you want your next left. I will let you know when."

"Where is this taking us?"

"Well, it looks like it's out by a bunch of ponds. The roads are weird. Half of them don't even have names."

Marc drove for several minutes. The terrain was hilly and dark. He was crawling along at less than 10 mph. The tree-lined street was desolate. The only light he could see was coming from his headlights. Route 6 had power, so Marc assumed a transformer must have blown nearby. With the power out, it was impossible to see any signs of life.

"OK, it's going to be up on the left," Chris said. "The next road."

Marc coasted again as they approached the turn. He came to a halt at a narrow opening of trees.

"This is a road?" Marc asked. "How the hell will my truck even fit through?"

"You'll be fine. We're almost there. Just follow this road down to the end and it will be on the right."

Marc turned the huge Dodge into the tight opening of trees. He winced as he heard the tree branches scratch along the sides of the truck. The dirt road under the snow was uneven and strewn with rocks. The Ram's suspension bottomed out as the tires sank into rough oversized holes.

The truck slowly made its way down the narrow road. Marc kept a tight grip on the wheel as the all-wheel-drive clawed its way through the snow and rocks. The tree coverage had thinned out, allowing more snow to reach the ground. He looked over at Chris. She was still looking intently at Tom's phone. He slowed down to a 5 mph crawl. The road slowly curved to the left.

"Wait," Chris said.

"What?"

"You passed it."

"How?"

"Back up."

Marc put the truck in reverse. He couldn't see anything behind him. His mirrors were clear, but the snowfall was so heavy it made everything a blur. As they moved backward, they came across an opening in the trees.

"Here," Chris said.

Marc stopped. He put the passenger window down so they could get a better look. It was an entrance to another road. The opening was even more constricted than the last one.

"What is this?" Marc asked. "A driveway?"

Chris zoomed in and out on the map image on the phone. It gave no indication of any other roads or buildings anywhere close by.

"I have no clue," Chris answered. She sighed in frustration as she swiped the image on the phone back and forth. "It's not on the map. But it has to be back there. Sitting in the middle of nowhere. We didn't pass any other roads, and we overshot the target on the map after we started turning left."

Marc could make out the indentation of fresh tire tracks in the snow leading down the driveway and into the darkness. Marc put the window back up, shifted the truck into Drive and turned right.

Chris and Marc remained silent as the truck slowly made its way down the long, winding path. The Ram's frame creaked in protest as it heaved up and down across the rutted, icy path. The snowfall briefly subsided as the trees surrounding them grew larger. The forest became dense, blacking out the sky above.

"There!" Chris said.

A flicker of light emerged from far beyond the trees. Marc continued to drive slowly, following the path as it snaked deeper into the woods. As they reached the end of the driveway, the trees parted, and they came to an opening. In front of them sat a huge Victorian house.

The house was in bad shape now, but it must have been stunning when it was new. Marc pegged the house for early 1800s. The foundation and façade around the main doors were stacked stone. A huge covered porch wrapped across the front and right side of the house. The giant wooden posts supporting the porch were quite old and weathered, and the roof was sagging at the corners. Although the roof's shingles were covered in snow, it was obvious that there were several places where there were missing shingles. Snow and rain were most likely leaking into the structure.

"Wow," Chris said. "That's a big house. Can you imagine what that renovation project would be like?"

"Actually, I can," Marc said. A grin spread across his face as he briefly considered how he would repair the house. "See Babe, this is what we should be doing out here. You find these houses, and I renovate them. We would be unstoppable."

Another text from Julie.

I'm freaking out here. What's up, Becker?

Chris was now annoyed.

Getting it now. Will text when heading home. Stop bothering us, Perez!

As they rolled closer to the house, they noticed there were only two lights emanating from inside. One came from a dimly lit corner room on the second floor. Sheer lace curtains diffused whatever might be inside. But the light and shadows wavered, indicating the room was most likely lit by a candle. The ground floor was pure darkness except for a sliver of light spilling out of the back corner. There was a vehicle parked to the right of the porch. It was the old Jeep that had been at the store.

"Bingo," Chris said, pointing to it.

Marc parked in the middle of the driveway.

"Let's make this quick," he said. "And remember, you need to be the one to apologize."

Marc and Chris stepped out into the cold. Chris shoved her hands into her pockets to hold her coat close to her body. It was too cold to attempt to zip it up, and she didn't feel like putting her gloves on. The wind gusts had finally died down a bit.

Marc noticed a second vehicle on the side of the house. It looked to be another Jeep. A Wrangler. This one had huge studded off-road tires and a winch kit. It was old but fairly customized. *Tommy would love that*, Marc thought to himself.

"What's going on back there?" Chris asked. She pointed past the Wrangler to a barn set far back behind the main property. Towering trees surrounded it. The building was in worse shape than the house. Its massive front door was ajar, and light spilled out into the yard. The light, obviously from a fire, danced unevenly across the drifting snow. A pig wandered out of the door, looked around, and went back inside.

"Even the pigs hate this weather," Chris said. Chris took

one last look at the app to confirm they were in the right place. She showed it to Marc. "Front door?"

"Come on," Marc replied.

Marc and Chris walked toward the front entrance. The front steps were cracked and rotted in sections, so they walked on the edges to avoid breaking the treads.

Once under the roof of the porch, they dusted snow from their shoulders. The natural-wood front door had three large stained-glass panels, one across the top, and one on each side. The glass was a mix of amber-, rose- and olive-colored squares, intersected by dark blue roundels. Matching glass panels ran down either side of the entire doorframe. The inner hallway was dark, making it impossible to see inside.

Marc pressed the doorbell and waited. After twenty seconds, he looked at Chris, shrugged, and pushed it again.

"I didn't even hear it ring," Chris said. "It's probably broken like everything else in this dump."

Chris stepped forward and pounded on the door, banging on the wide piece of wood that bisected the two long glass panels.

"Chris!" Marc yelled in objection.

"What?"

They waited several seconds.

"We should have waited a bit longer," Marc said. "That was rude."

"I don't want to stand here freezing my ..."

A small orange glow appeared at the end of the hallway. It grew larger as it got closer to the front door. The light settled in place behind one of the side panes of stained glass. Someone's face pressed against the glass above it.

After a brief pause, a metal clunk rang out as the door unlocked. Slowly, it creaked open. A petite, older woman, shorter than Tom and Julie, stuck her head out. Her silver hair was pulled back into a bun. Gray and white strands fell haphazardly around her neck. A pair of reading glasses attached to a silver chain hung low across her chest. She looked to be in her mid-60's.

"Can I help you?" asked the old woman.

"Hi," Marc said. "Our friend left his backpack at your

candle store earlier."

The woman stood motionless, her head still jutting out from behind the door. The front of her left foot stuck out a bit onto the porch, exposing a worn, faded blue slipper. She used her other foot to stop the door from blowing open. Her expression did not change.

"Well, I'm assuming it was your store," Marc continued. "Out on Route 6 in Truro? The little brown house buried beneath the pine trees? I recognize the Jeep from it."

"Oh, yes, the bag," the woman said. She squinted as she looked at Marc. The candle in the hallway was not providing much light for her to see. "How did you know where to find it?"

Chris held up the phone so the woman could see the map. She pulled her glasses up and leaned in closer to study it.

"There is a tablet in the backpack," Chris said. "They sort of talk to each other, so we were able to use the phone to find the tablet."

"You kids and your toys today."

The old woman stepped back and removed her glasses.

"Well, this makes things much easier," she said as she opened the door.

There was a candle on a small table next to the front doorway. Marc noticed it was the same squared-off glass jar design as the one from the store. The old woman picked the candle up and led them down a long hallway toward the back of the house, scuffing her slippers along the way.

There was a dim light at the end of the hallway. To the right of them was a giant dining room. To the left was an even bigger living room. All the lights were off, making it difficult to see what was in each room, but Marc made out a huge fireplace up against the far wall of the living room.

The floorboards creaked as they made their way down the hall. They passed a long wooden staircase with intricate details carved into the banister posts and railing.

The soles of the woman's slippers flopped up and down between the bottom of her feet and the floor. At the end of the hallway, the woman turned right. As he was about to turn into the kitchen, Marc heard another floorboard creak, but this one from upstairs. He glanced back at the staircase before following Chris into the room.

Although not original to the house, the spacious kitchen hadn't been updated in at least forty years. Simple pine cabinets were painted 1970s harvest gold. The butcher-block countertops were riddled with stains and scratches from decades of use. The counters were cluttered with various pots, pans, and containers. A cookbook sat open on the counter beside an old gas stove.

There was a door that led out to the side porch. A large double-paned window sat above the sink, overlooking the backyard. The barn was visible through the window. It was much closer from this corner of the house. The old window rattled from the wind.

In the middle of the room sat a large rectangular metal kitchen table and six chrome stools, their seats wrapped in turquoise vinyl. Most were torn and cracked. Two huge candles sat in the middle of the kitchen table.

Marc noticed Tom's backpack sitting at the end of the table.

"So, is the woman from the store here?" Marc asked. "We'd really like to apologize to her. Can we see her?"

Another creak, this one longer and deeper, descended from upstairs. Chris glanced up and then over at Marc. The old woman put her candle on the counter next to the stove and walked to the table. She dragged a chair out and groaned slightly as she slowly sat down.

"No," the woman replied. After a brief pause, she continued. "That was my daughter, Sara. She's ... busy."

Marc was beginning to feel uncomfortable. Even though she was a petite woman, he felt threatened, and not the least bit welcome. Neither did Chris. She could sense the tension in the room.

"Chris Becker, realtor," Chris said, flashing her ultra-white smile and extending her hand. "And you are?"

"Tired."

The old woman sat hunched over and did not accept Chris' hand. The smile quickly faded from Chris' face. *Yup, she's the mother.* She took a few steps back to be closer to Marc.

"Sara told me all about you kids and what happened at the

store today," she continued. "Such disrespect. You caused a lot of damage. Do you know how long it took to make those candles?"

"Well, that's the other reason we're here," Marc said.

"She also told me that the girl was asking a lot of questions about some urban legends. I don't know how much my daughter told you, but the legend you hear today is nothing like what really happened."

The old woman got up from the table and walked over to the stove. There was a faded copper teakettle on top. She picked it up and shook it to gauge the amount of water in it. She put it back down and grabbed a match from the box sitting on the counter next to the stove. She lit the match, and then turned the burner on to ignite the gas.

"Tea?" she asked.

"No, thank you," Marc said. *Why is she changing the conversation?*

The old woman turned toward Marc and Chris. She leaned back against the counter next to the stove and folded her arms.

"Death descended upon this home about thirty years ago," she continued. "Or was it forty? It's been so long."

She frowned as she tried to remember the date.

"Murder," she continued. "It happened right here. Well, back in the barn, actually. That's where we make the candles. My husband, God rest his soul, had taken in this drifter. I had objected to it at the time. My husband was always more trusting than I was. Well, he was at the beginning. To me, trust is something that is earned. Do you know what I mean?"

The old woman shot Chris a long stare.

"Sure," Marc said.

She walked over to a row of faded blue tin jars along the back of the counter, opened one, and removed a tea bag. The corner cabinet had a glass door on it. She opened it and removed a tiny cup and saucer.

"So, I tell this drifter that he is going to have to earn his keep. No freeloading around here."

The woman's voice was growing louder and her gestures more excitable as she continued her story. She walked back to the stove and turned off the burner just as the water began to boil.

"He was here for about a week when he betrayed that trust," she continued. The old woman shook her head in disgust as she began to pour the hot water into her cup. "It's just so awful when you try to show kindness to strangers, and in return, they show nothing but disrespect. As God as my witness, I'll never understand such behavior."

She turned and gave Chris another long stare. Slowly, she walked back over to the kitchen table and sat down with her tea.

"We really can't stay too long," Marc said.

"Well, I don't want to get into the details because they are just too ... upsetting. I had never seen such hate and rage explode upon innocence. Things got so violent so quickly. There was so much blood. So much ... death. The bodies that collapsed onto that hay-covered floor ..."

She paused and turned to look out the window at the barn.

"You have to protect those you hold most dear. You have to at least try. You understand, don't you?"

Marc and Chris stared at her in silence. She continued to look out through the ice-covered window toward the barn. Marc began to tense up. This woman was mentally unstable, struggling to pull the pieces of the past together.

"I lost the man I loved that night. I really did. Sometimes it feels like it all happened just the other day. It plays over and over in my head. At other times, it feels like a lifetime ago."

The old woman glanced down and stared into her tea, lost in her thoughts.

"And my Sara. My poor Sara was just beside herself. She was only twelve when it happened. That's too young to lose so much. Witnessing death at such a young age is something that stays with you. Especially when the trauma involves your twin sister. My poor Sara ... She takes after her father, you know. Quite the hot head, that one."

Chris didn't realize how badly she was wringing her hands together. This story had her completely intrigued. Part of her wanted to run. Part of her wanted to hear more. Chris looked over at Marc. She expected to find him staring intently at the old woman just like she was, but instead he was looking directly at her. She wondered how long he had been staring.

He mouthed the words "we are leaving."

"I'm so sorry for your loss," Marc said as he turned to face the old woman. "We really need to be going. That storm outside is only going to get worse."

The old woman looked up from her tea somewhat startled as if awoken from a dream. She looked over at Marc and Chris and frowned. The floorboards upstairs once again let out a long, drawn-out creak.

"Would you like to see the barn before you go?" the old woman asked.

"Really?" Chris said. "That might be ..."

"No," Marc replied. "We really need to go. Can you do me a favor and give this to your daughter?" Marc placed five $20 bills on the table in front of the woman. "I hope that covers the candles. I tried to pay her at the store, but she wouldn't take the money. It's all the cash I have."

The old woman looked at the pile of money on the table and frowned.

"There is always a price to be paid," she said sternly.

Marc stepped forward and picked up Tom's backpack and flung it over his shoulder.

"Chris, I believe you have something to say as well," Marc said.

Chris was confused. She wasn't ready to leave. She wanted to hear the details about what happened in the barn. But the look on Marc's face said it was time to go.

"Oh, yes ... um, sorry," Chris said. "I'm sorry. Truly, I am. It was an accident. I didn't mean to break the candles."

The old woman squinted at Chris and grimaced.

"We are all very sorry," Marc added.

Marc grabbed Chris by the shoulder and spun her toward the hallway. They quickly made their way to the front door. As they reached it, Marc looked back over his shoulder. The old woman was not following. He looked up the staircase to see if Sara was there, but all he saw was darkness. The creaking had stopped. He turned the old brass knob on the front door, and he and Chris stepped out onto the dilapidated porch. Marc slammed the door behind him. He and Chris walked over to his truck. The winds had died down a little, but the snow was falling faster than it had been when they arrived. Marc paused at the door of his truck and began to dust off the snow-covered windows. Chris stopped a few feet behind Marc and turned to look back at the old building behind the house.

"What's the rush?" Chris asked. "I want to go see that barn."

"Are you serious? You've had too much to drink, Babe. Focus! Chris that woman was disturbed. That story she was telling, it was ..."

"It was way more interesting than the one in that stupid book Julie has. A real murder happened back there! How cool is that?"

Marc stopped clearing the windows of his truck and turned to face Chris. He dropped Tom's knapsack in front of the driver's door.

"Something was off," Marc said. "About all of it. She seemed really confused. And that house. Who was upstairs? Didn't you hear the floorboards creaking? I assumed it was Sara, but that old woman said she wasn't around."

"No, she said she was busy. She's probably just mad at us. Do you think she's in the barn? Maybe we should go look. Do you think the hay is still covered in blood after so many decades?"

Chris turned to walk toward the barn. Marc grabbed her and yanked her back, grabbing her by the shoulders.

"There are two Jeeps here," Marc continued. "I seriously doubt that old bat could drive either one of them. She looks as frail as a pile of matchsticks. Sara has to be in the house. Maybe someone else is here if there are two cars. And what about that veiled threat as we were leaving? This doesn't feel right. We need to go, Babe. Now!"

Marc glanced back toward the barn. It sat dark and ominous beneath several large trees. He turned and looked past Chris, and then up to the second floor of the house. The flickering light of a candle still danced against the front corner window. But now, behind the lace curtains, stood a backlit figure looking down on them. He loosened his grip on Chris. Marc couldn't tell who it was. The figure slowly walked away from the glass. Seconds later, the light went off.

"I just thought it would be cool to see where she said that murder happened," Chris said. "Maybe Sara is back there and I can apologize in person."

"Chris, I don't want to start an argument about this, OK? Why won't you listen to me?"

"Seriously? All I ever do is listen to you. Because all you ever do is tell me what I'm supposed to do! Stop trying to run my life!"

"What's that supposed to mean?"

Chris sighed. She didn't want another fight. She reached into her coat pocket and took out her case with the Gucci glasses. *Maybe we use the drive home to talk about our future?* Chris thought to herself.

A huge blast of wind sliced between Chris and Marc. Chris dug her hands into her coat pockets and pulled her arms tight across her chest. She looked over at Marc and then down at the snow-covered ground. The wind eventually subsided.

Chris removed her glasses from the case and wiped the lenses on her sleeve. She tucked the case back into her coat pocket and looked up into Marc's big brown eyes. The grip Marc had on her shoulders suddenly felt very confining.

"Marcus, listen ..." Chris said.

Before Chris could continue, an arrow tip exploded through her left shoulder, piercing her scapula and ripping through the front of her leather jacket. Her glasses fell to the ground. Chris grabbed onto Marc's arms for balance. Marc looked on in horror as Chris howled in pain. Blood quickly began to seep across the front of her white sweater. Marc stared in disbelief at the arrowhead that was sticking through Chris' jacket. It was a triple-bladed tip. The unique kidney-shaped cutouts in the blade were identical to the one from the store.

"Marc!" Chris screamed.

Marc looked around in a panic. His heart was pounding hard inside his chest. And then he began to focus. *Where is she?* He took a deep breath, paused, and looked up to the corner window on the second floor. The light was still out, but the window was now open. The faded lace curtains were blowing back and forth in the wind.

A second arrow emerged from the blackness of the corner

room. It whizzed through the icy air, piercing Chris' right boot and fastening her foot to the ground. Her leg buckled and she fell to one knee, shrieking in pain.

"Marc!" Chris screamed. "Help! What the hell is happening? Marc! Help me!"

Marc tried to lift Chris, but she pushed him away from her, howling in protest. The arrow had sliced through her foot and straight into the ground beneath her, pinning her in place. She couldn't free herself. She could feel the shaft of the arrow rubbing against her raw flesh.

"My foot!" Chris cried. "Stop! I can't move it. I can't ... help ... help me, Marc! Help me! Please!"

Marc looked at the arrow jutting out from her boot. The bright yellow fletchings vibrated in the wind.

How can I remove this so I can get her into the truck?

Before he could think of a solution, another arrow tore through the blistering cold night, striking Marc dead-center in his chest.

He staggered backward, falling against the side of his truck. As he slid to the ground, he heard the tip of the arrow grind against the truck's door. The tip gouged the bright white "Sirola Construction" sign, smearing it with blood. Marc couldn't breathe. He lifted his head from the ground to see Chris struggling to keep her balance.

She faltered, and her right ankle snapped as she fell to the ground.

A hand pulled back the faded lace curtains and shut the window. The front door opened, and the old woman stepped out into the stormy night. Snow crunched under Mother's faded blue slippers as she calmly walked to the two bloodied bodies lying in the snow. She knelt by Marc's side and smiled.

TWELVE

Storm

It had been over an hour since Tom and Julie last heard from Chris. Julie glanced at her phone. The display showed it was a few minutes before 7 p.m., and her battery charge had dropped to fifteen percent. She unlocked her phone to send another message.

> Sorry to bother you, but it is getting late.
> Everything OK?

"I just sent a text to your phone," Julie said. "I'm seriously starting to freak out a bit. They left two hours ago. All we get is silence. Why aren't you worried?"

Tom was busy in the kitchen cleaning up from the dinner they'd just finished.

"Maybe they decided to go to the hardware store in Wellfleet while they were out that way. I wouldn't worry just yet. Did you try texting Chris or Marc directly?"

"Shit. No. See, that's why I have you to think of these things!"

She first sent a message to Chris.

Haven't heard back. What's up?

She then immediately tried Marc.

Are you on your way back?

"OK, so I sent messages to all three phones. One of them has to respond."

"I can understand Marc not responding," Tom said. "He's driving. But what's up with the silent treatment from Chris?"

"I think she felt we were nagging them. She also doesn't like being told what to do."

"Then she shouldn't be dating Marc. He can be a bit ... bossy at times."

"Oh my God!" Julie cried.

"What? Did you get a text?"

"No. I didn't tell you about my talk with Chris! I think she's going to dump Marc."

"Again? Well they are shifting from monthly to practically weekly events, aren't they?"

"No, I mean the big dump. Forever."

Tom turned off the lights in the kitchen and checked to make sure that the counters had been wiped clean. He headed to the sectional and sat across from Julie.

"Wait. Talk? What talk?"

"When you and Marc went grocery shopping. We had some cocktails and she sort of vented about Marc and everything. Long story short, she feels it is way too soon for her to settle down with anyone. Apparently, the blowout after game night was epic. Worse than Marc told us. She was done. She loves the real estate world that Marc has opened up for her, but she's just not ready."

"So I was right? She's been using him."

Julie frowned as she took a sip of her espresso martini.

"You two are actually a lot alike, you know. She's got a controlling dad."

"Please don't compare us."

Tom grabbed the last slice of cheese from the plate sitting

on the coffee table.

"Marc begged her to get back together," Julie said. "Maybe that's why they are so late. I bet they got in some fight or something. They're parked on the side of the road with some high drama lovers quarrel."

"You think this might be their final break up?" Tom asked with a smile.

"I'm positive."

Julie spent a moment studying Tom's overly joyous face.

"Why are you so happy?" Julie asked.

"I'm not."

Julie sat upright and leaned closer to Tom.

"Bullshit. I'm doing the math in my head, Tom, and I don't like how it adds up. Twice this weekend I've joked about you being jealous of Chris. Both times you've recoiled. Now you are practically beaming over the thought of them being permanently separated. Do you have some secret crush on Marc?"

"No!"

Tom got up and headed toward the kitchen, taking the empty plate of cheese with him.

"There you go again! I know that walk away move. You do have a crush! Spill it, Leblanc!"

Tom opened the fridge and removed the last package of cheese. He also grabbed the martini shaker off the top shelf. A quick rattle revealed it to be about half full. He brought both back over to the sectional.

"I don't have a crush on Marc, Jewels."

Julie snatched the package of cheese from Tom and tore it open.

"But?"

Tom topped off their martini glasses and sat down by her side.

"OK. So, I have something to tell you. I know we normally share everything so please spare me the lecture. Deal?"

Julie furrowed her brow as she looked Tom up and down.

"Go on."

"Do you remember the night we celebrated the completion of my kitchen remodel?"

Julie took a sip of her drink and nodded.

"Sure. You, me and Marc all had takeout."

"After you left Marc asked if he could shower. He said he had to stop off to see a client on the way home."

"Shower? What the ... Tom, I know where showers lead."

"I'm in my bedroom getting my stuff ready for the next day. Marc's in my shower. I hear the water turn off. The next thing I know his arms are around me. He is wet and naked."

"Oh my God! How could you have kept this from me?"

"He spins me around and says something about how adorable I am. I don't really remember. I was in so much shock. Before I know it, we start making out. Then ..."

"You gave him your flower?" Julie asked with a chuckle.

"No!"

"Well, what?"

"I ... I pushed him away."

"You what? Why?"

"I was drunk, Jewels! I panicked! I never saw it coming!"

"You are such an idiot! Then what?"

"I said something stupid like 'let's keep this professional.' I immediately regretted it. But it was too late. He quickly apologized and left."

"I can't believe you never told me this story!"

"Because I knew you would start to judge me."

"I'm about to!"

"There's no point, Jewels. Look, I'm not in love with him. I'm not carrying some torch for him. I just ... Marc's amazing. I compare every guy I meet to him. Nobody measures up. Every time he and Chris break up I think maybe I'll have a shot again."

"Sounds like a secret crush to me."

Julie took a chug from her glass. The alcohol burned the back of her throat. It relaxed her.

"Back this up for me," Julie said. "I thought Marc was straight."

"After I pushed him away I said the same thing to him. He told me he didn't see gender."

"Hunky stud say what now?"

"Those were his words, Jewels."

Tom sighed as ran his finger around the rim of his glass. He could feel Julie's eyes burrowing into him. He waited patiently for Julie to climb onto her soapbox.

"This is good," Julie finally said.

"What?" Tom asked. He looked over at Julie, somewhat surprised.

"They are breaking up. Forever! Chris was adamant! This totally explains why Marc is always taking your side. Always defending you."

"He does?"

"Seriously? You can be so blind sometimes. Look, Tom. Marc will be single very soon. He obviously cares for you. It all makes sense to me now. And he loves blondes! Oh my God, you two will make such a cute couple!"

"Jewels!" Tom began to laugh. "Stop."

"Give it time, Tom. Trust me. I'm the expert here. They are going to break up. That relationship is dead. Keep close to Marc. Drop some hints. Flirt. Tease. Then when the moment is right ..."

"Give him my flower?"

"Exactly!"

Tom and Julie both laughed. Julie let out a loud snort.

"Let's make it through tonight first, Jewels."

Julie held her glass up and nodded toward Tom. He held his up, and they clinked them together.

"One more thing," Julie said. "No more secrets. Agreed?"

"No more secrets."

***

Tom gazed at the items scattered across the dining room table. The flickering lights had prompted him and Julie to track down supplies they might need to deal with a power outage. They had a collection of votive candles, two books of matches, and a heavy-duty flashlight. Tom found the LED light most impressive. The sticker on the back rated it at 3000 lumens.

The lights in the condo wavered as the transformer at the top of the hill hummed in protest. Tom looked over at the clock on the microwave oven. It was 8 p.m.

"Anything yet?" Tom asked.

Julie glanced at her phone.

"Nothing. I told you I would hear it. My volume is maxed out. Can we turn the heat down? It's too hot in here. Can't we just build a fire if we lose power?"

"I looked at the fireplace earlier. I have no idea how to get it to work. I cranked the thermostat up because if we lose power we need to stay warm."

"I'm starting to feel like a baked turkey."

Tom surveyed the limited supplies on hand. He glanced back over at Julie. She was on the sectional with her face buried in her book.

"You need to stop with those urban legends."

"Tom, I know you think I'm crazy, but I really think that whack job at the store is tied to the story in this book."

"You're right, Jewels."

"I am?" Julie asked, surprised.

"Yes. I think you're crazy."

"Listen!" she said, scanning through the book's pages. "Here it is."

She lowered her voice.

> The ignorance displayed by the strangers only further enraged John's son. He found their contempt unforgivable. There was a price to be paid for such antipathy. That price was death.

Julie looked up to see Tom's reaction.

"Don't you find it just a bit *too* similar to what happened at the store?" Julie asked. "I mean, that woman all but said those same words to us."

"I'll admit, there is a similarity, Jewels."

"The legend never names the killer. But his reaction is just like that woman's."

"If you had never read that book, would you even be sitting here worried that the crazy lady at the store was anything more than a crazy lady? Would you really think she was a serial killer from some creepy old myth?"

"I guess ..."

The lights flickered again.

"Jewels, I hate to get all controlling on you, but out of curiosity how much juice is left on your phone? Because I haven't seen you plug that thing in all night."

Julie closed her book of legends and looked at her phone.

"Ugghhhh," Julie moaned. "I'm at six percent."

"Jewels!" Tom cried. "Plug it in!"

Julie leaped from the sectional and dashed over to the kitchen island. Her Zombunnies struggled as they tried to grip the slippery wood floor. She grabbed her cord and plugged it into the bottom of her phone. The phone suddenly rang out at full volume.

"It's about fucking time they called!" Julie exclaimed.

Her excitement quickly faded when she saw the name on the screen. She reluctantly answered the call.

"Hi, Mrs. Leblanc. Yes ... yes ... no. No, he's here with me ... uh huh ..."

Julie rolled her eyes in Tom's direction. He reached to grab the phone, but she blocked his hand with her arm.

"His phone has been acting up ... he hasn't been able to get a signal on it ... yeah, weird ... Of course, that's why that call ended earlier ... no ... no. He wouldn't have hung up on you. Sure ... hold on ..." Julie pressed the mute button. "Do *not* tell her what's going on," she warned as she passed the phone to Tom.

"Hey, Mom. Everything OK with you and Max?" He paused for several seconds before continuing. "I don't know what's going on with my phone. No signal or something. Must be the storm."

Tom sat in silence for three minutes while his mother admonished him for not checking in with her. He made a few futile attempts to get a word in with little success. Finally, she stopped talking.

"OK, I'm glad you're OK ... uh huh ... right ... no, we are fine. Still have power and everything. Yes ... yes, everyone is here safe."

"Everyone?" Julie whispered. "You just lied to her. I am *so* proud of you!"

Tom stifled a laugh.

"OK, let me get going ... OK ... yes ... I ... I love you, too."

Tom ended the call and immediately plugged the phone into an outlet on the kitchen island.

"She does not shut up," Tom said. "Please tell me I am not that bad."

"God no. Don't worry. I'll never let you get that annoying."

"Thanks, Jewels."

"So how are things back home?"

"She said they are already at two feet of snow. Snowdrifts are over four feet."

"Holy shit."

"She hasn't lost power yet, but about a third of the state has. Lots of places in western Massachusetts are out as well. But she stocked up on mountains of food and water, so I know she and Max will be fine."

"Well, that was a long phone call if everything is fine."

"You know how she is. She's just pissed that I'm not there."

"You can't spend the rest of your life being there for her."

"She needs me, Jewels. She's got nobody else."

Julie pulled her phone closer and nervously tapped her finger against the glass front.

"Tom ... I ... I know you don't like talking about your dad's death."

Tom made his way to the opposite side of the island, putting some distance between him and Julie.

"I didn't know you back then," Julie continued. "It was years before we met. You were only twelve, right? After that, it became just you and your mom. You had to grow up overnight. I get that. But at some point, you have to let go. You have to move on. You can't remain the man of the house forever."

"I know, Jewels. Living on my own, in a different city, has definitely helped. But she will always be my mom. She will always need me. I have to be there for her. I wasn't for him. When my dad needed me most, I ..."

Tom stared out the ice-covered window and watched the snow blow across the glass panes. Julie walked over to his side and took his hand.

"What happened that night, Tom? I know you were there. But nothing more than that. We said no more secrets."

The lights flickered. The microwave started to beep.

"I'll reset it," Tom said.

The transformer on the utility pole at the top of the driveway suddenly let out a shower of sparks. A loud pop emanated from it as the ice-covered power lines collapsed to the ground. Seabreeze Village was plunged into permanent darkness.

THIRTEEN

Birthday

2001 Friday 20-Jan 11:25 p.m.

Paul Leblanc closed the novel he was reading and glanced toward the open doorway. The foyer was pitch black. He leaned forward and cocked his head sideways, aiming his left ear at the door. He waited a few seconds before he heard it. A very faint scraping sound was coming from somewhere in the house.

Paul placed the book on the table next to his chair. He gripped the leather arms, and cautiously returned his recliner to its upright position. The coil springs in the old chair remained silent. He quietly exhaled a sigh of relief.

Once again, Paul heard the distinct sound of metal and glass grinding against one another. He determined it was coming from the back of the house. His heart began to beat faster.

What is that? Paul wondered.

The closet door on the opposite side of the den looked to be a mile away. Paul tiptoed over to the door and slowly turned the handle until he heard it unlatch. As he opened the door, the upper hinge let out a long, loud creak. He stopped.

Shit.

Paul continued to open the door, pulling it as slowly as possible to prevent the hinge from making any more sounds. Once the door was open, he looked at the locked safe inside and exhaled. He took a couple of steps back and began to check his pockets. Paul glanced around the room. His eyes darted from the table to the bookcase and back.

Where are my keys?

Another scraping sound emanated from down the hallway. This one was even louder than the last.

No keys.

Paul looked around the room again. His gaze settled on a dark gray stone statue sitting on the ledge of the bay window. It was a man and woman, wrapped in one another's arms, kissing. He had bought it for his wife as an anniversary gift five years ago when they were on vacation in Mexico. The bottom of the statue had an inscription on it -- The Lovers.

Paul grabbed the statue by the pair's entwined torso. He guessed the weight to be around ten pounds or so.

This will have to do.

The hallway to the back of the house was dark. Paul stood in the foyer and glanced at the staircase that led to the second floor. A faint light came from the Tiffany lamp sitting on the table at the landing at the top of the stairs. It cast just enough light onto the maple wood floor in the hallway so that Paul could see where he was walking. He warily made his way toward the kitchen.

As Paul reached the end of the hall, he took a position opposite the entrance to the kitchen. He noticed the light over the stove was still on.

I turned that off over an hour ago.

Paul raised the statue over his head, took a deep breath, and vaulted into the kitchen.

"Hi, Dad," Tom said with a big grin.

Paul abruptly came to a halt and stared in disbelief. His son was sitting at the far end of the kitchen table, quietly enjoying a slice of birthday cake. The glass plate was smeared with a white cream frosting.

"Tommy!"

Tom's smile faded as he looked at the statue in his father's hand. The grimace on his face told Tom he was in trouble.

"What?" Tom asked, somewhat confused.

"You scared the shit out of me! What are you doing up?"

"You said shit!" Tom chuckled at his dad's cursing.

Tom grabbed his fork and collected frosting from the edges of the plate before sliding it into his mouth. The screech of the fork against the glass plate was loud and irritating.

"Sorry. I wanted another piece of cake."

Paul let out a nervous laugh as he made his way over to the table. He rested the statue at the end and sat down next to his son. Tom smiled again as he continued to enjoy the buttery white frosting.

"The cake is that good?" Paul asked.

"Definitely. It's better than Mom's!"

Paul laughed and ran his hand across his son's long wavy blond hair.

"Well don't tell your mother that. You know her carrot cake recipe is a family secret. She would go postal if she knew you preferred this one. I grabbed it last minute from the bakery."

"It'll be our secret, Dad."

"I'm sorry she couldn't be here. She's sorry too."

"I know."

Tom looked over at the French door that led out to the backyard. The glass panes were covered in snow and ice.

"Do you think the weather will clear by tomorrow?" Tom asked.

"The storm should be done by morning. I'm sure they'll have the airports open soon after that. She will definitely be home this weekend."

Tom stared at the statue sitting on the far end of the table.

"What's that for?" Tom asked.

"I didn't know you were in here. I thought someone may have been trying to break in. You know there have been a series of robberies lately."

"I know."

"I didn't have my key to the gun case. I had to improvise."

Tom dragged his index finger across the few remaining

streaks of frosting. Paul grinned as he watched his son polish off the last remnants of his late-night snack.

"OK mister, you need to get back upstairs. We have a long day of shoveling to do tomorrow. Who knows how much snow this storm will drop on us."

Tom walked over to the counter and placed his fork and plate in the sink. He was about to lick his fingers when he noticed the knife resting on the edge of the sink. It was covered in frosting and bits of carrot cake. He gently ran his fingers across the edge and collected one final taste of birthday bliss.

"Are you staying up?" Tom asked as he licked his fingers one last time.

"I'll be up in a bit. I want to double check all of the doors to make sure we are locked up. And I forgot to turn the outside lights on as well. Go to bed."

As Tom walked past his dad, Paul reached out and pulled on the sleeve of his son's pajamas. Tom stopped and turned.

"Happy birthday, Tommy. We'll do gifts when your mom is here."

Tom grinned, ran into the hallway and quickly bounded upstairs to his bedroom.

***

The sound of shattering glass woke Tom from his sleep. He glanced at the clock next to his bed. It was 2 a.m. He stared at his bedroom door waiting to see if it would open. His heart began to race. The house was silent for several moments. Another crash. Tom decided to investigate. He leaped from his bed and cautiously opened his door.

His dad was at the top of the staircase, holding a phone in one hand and his key ring in the other. He was wearing blue and gray flannel pajama bottoms and a white t-shirt.

"Dad, what's ..." Tom began to ask.

"Back to bed," Paul whispered. "Do not leave that room!"

Tom swiftly closed the door and ran back to his bed, diving under the covers. He made a small opening in the sheets so that he could keep an eye on the door.

Tom stared at his clock. 2:01 a.m. He listened for

something. Anything. The house was silent. It was now 2:02 a.m. The minutes felt like hours as they passed by.

The silence abruptly ended. Tom heard a loud pop. He jumped from his bed and ran to his bedroom door. He lightly turned the knob and stuck his head out into the hallway. The faint sound of voices could be heard from downstairs. He could not make out what they were saying.

"Dad?" Tom whispered.

Tom waited for what felt like an eternity. There was no response. He opened his door and walked over to the top of the staircase. The voices from below could no longer be heard.

"Dad?" Tom whispered again.

Tom began to descend the stairs. The light from the front den was on. He walked in, hoping to find his dad there, but the recliner was empty. Tom noticed the closet door was open. He walked over to inspect it. The safe inside with his dad's gun was open. The safe was empty.

Tom spun around and looked at the bay window. The statue of The Lovers was sitting in its usual position. Tom ran over and grabbed it and walked out into the foyer. The light was off in the kitchen, but he could hear the table chairs sliding across the floor.

"Dad!" Tom called out as he ran down the hallway. He burst into the kitchen, stopping just a few feet into the room.

His father was bent over the table. A tall, powerful, hooded figure stood behind him, pinning him down by his neck. The light from the back porch spilled in through the glass panes of the French door. Tom watched as his dad reached out toward the end of the table. Tom realized his dad's gun was resting on the edge of the table. It was only a few feet away from Tom.

"Tommy," Paul called out, coughing and gasping for air.

Tom stood motionless. His eyes darted between the backlit figure, his father, and the gun. The sounds in the room faded away. All he could hear was the throbbing of his heart pounding deep within his chest.

"Dad?" Tom asked. His voice cracked with fear and confusion.

"Run!" Paul yelled.

Tom tried to turn but could not make his feet move. He felt

powerless.

The hooded intruder turned, grabbed the frosting cover knife off of the kitchen counter, and plunged it deep into the back of Paul Leblanc.

FOURTEEN

The Barn

Chris slowly opened her eyes. Her thoughts were a blur. She could barely see. *Where am I? What happened?*

It took all the strength she could muster to hold her head up straight. It ached from the alcohol she'd had earlier. Her temples pounded with every beat of her heart. She was parched. She tried to wipe her eyes, but her arms were immobilized, tied together behind her back.

What the ...? The memories came flooding back -- the argument, the howling storm, the house with the old woman, the pain in her shoulder, her foot in agony, grasping out to Marc for support.

Marc. Where is Marc?

Without her glasses, Chris could not focus on anything more than twenty feet away. She inhaled deeply, desperate to remain calm so she could assess her situation.

Chris was tied to a small chair. The narrow wooden seat was attached to a metal frame. A foldable desktop hung off the side of the chair. Her arms were pulled tightly behind her back. Her wrists bound together with a heavy rope. Each ankle was tethered to one of the chair's back legs so that her feet didn't touch the ground.

To her horror, she realized the first arrow, the one that had ripped through her shoulder, was still lodged in her body, its tip coated in deep-red blood.

Chris tried to move her legs to see if she could free them, but each movement sent a shooting pain throughout her body. She couldn't see the damage to her foot, but she could see the hole in her boot and the puddle of blood beneath it.

How long have I been like this?

The one thing Chris did know for certain was that she was in the barn. She recognized the giant arched door that was now slightly ajar.

The wind outside had intensified. The massive door rattled, its hinges creaking, as the wind pounded against it.

In front of Chris, several feet away, were two large tables, each roughly six-by-ten-feet wide and about three feet off the ground. The one to Chris' left had a stainless-steel top and wooden legs. It was partially covered by a large, badly stained tan tarp. It rustled as the breeze cut through the barn. Several hooks dangled from eyelets on its edges. They clinked softly as they banged against the sides of the table. The table's only contents were a roll of plastic bags and three glass jars.

The other table was made of solid wood. It had several knives of various shapes and sizes scattered on top of it, as well as two long saws. The knives all had a similar design on their wooden handles -- front and back spacers made of nickel along with inlaid turquoise.

Between the two tables, centered in the barn, was a giant iron cauldron. It stood roughly three feet tall and the same in diameter. Below it was a series of stacked stones that formed a huge fire pit. The heat from the fire was intense, but frigid temperatures and gusts of wind blowing in through the barn's door kept any of its warmth from reaching Chris.

She squinted, trying to get a better look at the inside of the barn. There were several gas lanterns hanging along the sidewalls. Only a few were lit. Chris could make out lines running to each lantern from a large white tank in the back corner of the barn.

There was also a loft in the back half of the barn, but it was not illuminated. Under it were a handful of stalls. A cow stood motionless in one of the stalls, quietly staring back at Chris. A set of giant tarps hung from the post at the end of the stalls.

In the very last stall, a carcass hung from a large hook attached to the ceiling. Chris shivered. It looked to be a cow carcass judging by its massive size, although it was hard to tell for sure. Its bones were bare save for tiny pieces of muscle that clung to them. The metal anchor and ceiling boards creaked from the weight of the cadaver as it rocked side to side in the wind.

Chris turned her gaze past the table to the other side of the barn. The dim lighting combined with her poor vision made it difficult for her to see anything over there. Additionally, the distortion from the heat, emanating from the fire pit, under the huge iron cauldron further obscured her vision. Whatever was in the pot was boiling and sending a lot of steam into the air. A brief, intense gust managed to momentarily clear her line of sight past the pot. Her heart immediately filled with joy at what she saw.

"Marc!" Chris yelled.

Marc didn't respond, but Chris' screams for him awakened a large Doberman that had been sleeping on the other side of the table closest to Chris. The dog growled as it emerged from behind the tarp, searching for the source of the noise that had disturbed its sleep. It stared at Chris, baring its long white fangs. The beast lunged at her, growling and snapping its jaws, desperate to reach its prey. And it would have if it weren't for a thick chain attached to its collar that yanked it to a halt just a few feet away from her.

"Christ!" Chris yelled.

The dog pulled hard at the chain, straining to break free to reach her.

"Marc!" Chris yelled again, squinting her eyes as she tried to see through the steam rising from the cauldron.

Marc sat motionless on the other side of the barn, unable to respond. He was tied to the same kind of chair that Chris was. His arms were behind his back. His legs, however, were covered with a tarp. The arrow that had pierced his chest had been removed, but his sweater and coat were drenched in blood.

"I can't get to you," Chris said. "Can you hear me?"

Chris was now fully awake and focused. The pain in her shoulder and foot was crippling, but the sight of Marc gave her a rush of adrenaline, and with it, a sense of hope.

I have to reach Marc!

A shadow suddenly cut across the barn floor to the right side of Chris, catching her off-guard. She turned to see a huge pig standing next to her. The creature stopped and looked right into Chris' eyes, snorting softly as it breathed.

What is this nightmare?

The pig turned and walked past Chris, cutting a path directly between her and the dog. The dog's eyes never took their gaze off Chris. The pig slowly made its way to the front door of the barn and stepped out into the storm.

"Focus, Chris!" Chris said aloud. "Think! Think!"

The barn's door groaned as the wind suddenly shifted. Then, another sound. Another door, this one in the back corner of the barn, beyond the stalls near the propane tank, had blown open. The wind had changed direction, and now frigid gusts were blasting Chris right in the face from the barn's rear.

That's when she noticed the stench. The wind had been at her back until now. This one came toward her. The last big gust had overwhelmed her with nausea.

What is that smell?

The huge iron pot was bubbling violently in the center of the barn. Chris remembered the carcass hanging from the stall at the back of the barn. The cow. The stench was coming from the mutilated remains.

The wind shifted back again. Chris took a deep breath of the cold crisp air. The lack of stench was refreshing, but gave her little comfort. Panic quickly washed over Chris.

"Marc, are you awake?"

Chris' eyes darted around the perimeter of the old barn. She was desperate to escape. Her right leg was useless. Her left leg was bound incredibly tight. But there was the slightest amount of slack in the rope around her wrists. She had to make it work. Chris began to slowly twist her hands back and forth. She continued to look around the building, checking the exits to be sure she was still alone. Her eyes came to rest, focusing on a post several feet away from Marc, visible past the opposite side of the pot.

Two more people, covered from the neck down by tarps. Chris squinted, trying to bring their faces into focus. A man and a woman, both with dark hair.

How many will I have to save?

The dog growled as Chris struggled to free her wrists. Ever so slightly the rope began to loosen.

"Marc, I don't know if you can hear me. But I am going to get us out of here," she said. "I know I screwed up. This is all my fault. All of it. You've always been the one to fix things. To make things right. Always. This time it's up to me. OK? Do you hear me? Marc!"

Marc did not respond. Chris' eyes burned with tears.

"You were right. OK?" She cried. "I'm sorry I'm such a stubborn ass. I know you only want what's best for me. I know that you want us to build a life together because you love me. I love you, too. I do. I know I don't say it that often, but I do. I promise I am going to get us out of this. Everything is going to work out. Everything. I promise."

Chris took a deep breath, closed her eyes, and focused on freeing her wrists. Slowly she slid them back and forth, in and out, back and forth, in and out, over and over again.

FIFTEEN

Blackout

Tom and Julie were seated on opposite sides of the sectional, wrapped in blankets from the upstairs guest bedroom. The temperature in the condo had dropped several degrees in the past few hours. Outside, the wind gusts were now over 50 mph; not as strong as they had been in Providence, but still strong enough to deliver a powerful blow to the Outer Cape.

A bit of warmth emanated from the kitchen. Tom had managed to light the front two burners of the gas stove to help throw a small amount of heat into the adjoining space.

Julie and Tom sat in silence. Several small votive candles cast a dim light throughout the rooms. They had placed two on the kitchen island, one in the bathroom, two on the dining room table, and the final three on the coffee table in the living room. One by one, they were slowly burning out.

Julie glanced at her phone. 9:30 p.m. with three percent battery charge remaining.

"I'm so pissed that I didn't think to charge my phone earlier," Julie said.

"If we had my backpack, we could just use that big power charger I told you about. The whole reason I got that was for situations just like this."

"Well, if we had your pack, we wouldn't be sitting here waiting for them to return."

Tom turned his head so he could see out of the big side window in the living room. Sections of the glass panes were caked in ice. He was hoping to see a set of headlights illuminate the trees and shrubs at the top of hill, but there was nothing but darkness.

"I'm really getting worried, Jewels."

"Well, it's about fucking time. I've been worried for hours!"

"The thing is, they've got three phones. So even if one of the phones died, there's no reason for them not to contact us."

"Well, maybe there isn't cell service."

"Truro is not that far away, and we still have service. I would think they would too."

Julie looked at her phone to confirm she still had a signal. It was a very weak one, but it was there.

"What should we do?" Julie asked.

"What *can* we do, Jewels?" Tom felt helpless.

Julie stared up at the ceiling, lost in her thoughts, going over the events that had transpired back at the candle store. The sound of the glass countertop shattering had shaken her to the core. It rang in her head repeatedly.

"Well, one thing I know I'm going to do when we get back home is take up kickboxing," Julie said.

"Really?" Tom looked over at her. She was still staring up at the ceiling.

"Really. I think Marc was right about the fight or flight thing. It would be good for me to learn to defend myself. How about you? Maybe we can do it together? Oh, at the same time! Marc is so big I bet even with both of us ganging up on him he would still kick our asses!"

Tom rolled over and pulled the blanket higher around his head to cover his ears.

"I don't know," Tom replied. "I know Marc wants me to get back to kickboxing, but it was really awkward for me. I'm not ... I'm not really a fighter. I just didn't like it."

"Probably because you were punching a guy you were attracted to," Julie said with a laugh.

"Can we not go back down that road?"

"Sorry."

"Actually, when Marc and I were at the store I promised him I would give archery a try."

"Archery?" Julie asked, surprised. She turned her head and looked over at Tom. "Where the hell did that come from?"

"Marc found an archery arrow in the store. He told me it would help me with my confidence. Said there was an archery range up in Lincoln he wanted to take me to."

"And will you go?"

"I told him yes, but that was sort of just to shut him up."

"Seriously, Tom?" Julie sat up straight and glared at Tom across the table. "What is wrong with you?"

"I know. I probably really should, shouldn't I?

"Why wouldn't you? Marc's right. That sounds like it would be perfect for you. Hand-eye coordination. Balance. Calmness. And like he said, a total confidence-builder. Plus, it might help you get your mother out of your blood."

"What's that supposed to mean?"

"Remember in the drive out here? You were so focused on trying to play navigator from the back seat that you never bothered to have fun."

"I was having fun!"

"No, you were stressing. You need to learn to relax, Tom. Enjoy the ride. Just like Marc said. Remember?"

"I ... I guess. Maybe. Would you want to try archery with us?"

"No. Sounds kind of boring."

"Thanks a lot."

"I meant for me, not you."

"Besides, I really want to learn to kick ass. I kind of froze at the store when that lady freaked out."

"We all did."

Julie turned and looked out the glass panels in the side door next to the kitchen. The covered porch protected it from the buildup of snow. She could still see the snow falling heavily outside of the townhouse. The huge window to the right was half covered with ice.

"I'm tired, but I don't want to go to bed," Julie said. "I feel like if we do, we're sort of giving up on them."

"Ditto on that, Jewels. But that raging fire on the stovetop is not doing much to keep this place warm. Heat rises, so we're probably better off upstairs. Besides, these candles are just about done."

Julie swung her legs out from under her blanket and dropped her Zombunnies onto the floor. She sat upright and looked around the condo. The votive in the bathroom had gone dark, as had the ones in the dining room.

"Agreed," Julie said.

Tom leaned forward and blew out the two candles that were still burning in the living room. He flicked on the heavy metal flashlight he had been keeping by his side. Julie walked into the kitchen and turned off the burners on the stove. The window over the sink howled slightly from the ice-cold wind pounding against it. She turned to blow out the last votive, but it went out by itself. There was a book of matches on the counter next to the stove. She picked it up.

"I'm drained, Tom," Julie said. She walked back to the sectional and grabbed her blanket and headed toward the staircase at the back of the condo.

"I want to double-check all the doors. Hold on a minute."

"I'm fine," Julie said, stretching her arms above her head and yawning. "I'll see you upstairs."

"Take the flashlight."

Tom aimed the beam over at Julie and focused on her face. She held up her hands to block it.

"Oh my God, that is way too bright!"

"Sorry," Tom said. He lowered the light down and away from her face.

"I'm fine. I have night vision. Well, I did until you blinded me."

Julie grabbed the railing and looked up into the darkness at the top of the staircase. She really had been momentarily blinded by the flashlight and needed to give her eyes a few seconds to adjust. Step by step, she slowly made her way up the stairs, sliding each bunny-covered foot against the back riser to help her gauge the spacing. Once at the top of the stairs, she turned into the bedroom.

The light washing in from the huge, arched window barely illuminated the room. It provided enough light so she could find her way to the bed. She tossed the blanket across the mattress and looked out into the backyard. The snow was falling fast and heavy. The trees along the back of the property were completely enshrouded in snow and ice. She pressed her hand to the window and wondered where Marc and Chris were, and if they were safe.

***

Tom swallowed two ibuprofen with a big glass of water. It was his anti-hangover mixture. He had failed to do it the night before and did not want to wake up with another foggy headache.

He walked over to the hallway and twisted the deadbolt on the front door back and forth to confirm it was locked. As he made his way through the kitchen, he double-checked the stove to make sure Julie hadn't accidentally left the burners on when she'd turned them off. She hadn't.

He checked the side door, then continued toward the French door in back, stopping to look through the big side window in the living room. The bottom half of the window was encrusted in snow and ice. But he was able to see through the top half. The Seabreeze Village sign was swinging in the wind. It was dark now; the landscape lighting was out.

He made his way to the French door and jiggled the deadbolt. They were safely secured.

Tom went back to the sectional, grabbed his blanket and tossed it over his shoulder. He used his flashlight to guide him up the staircase. As he reached the top of the stairs, he noticed a light coming from the bedroom. Julie was in her bed, using the light on her phone to read by.

"Jewels!"

"What?"

"You're going to kill your battery."

Tom aimed the flashlight at Julie.

"Keep that out of my face. That thing is seriously powerful."

Tom tilted the flashlight down toward the floor.

"I was going through my urban legend book," Julie said. "I'm reading the story again. The one about that candle legend from Wellfleet."

"You are way too obsessed with that story."

"In the book, the guy kills a brother and sister because they disrespected him," Julie said. "He had a cart set up on his farm. It had homemade cheese from their goats. They thought it tasted awful. The sister actually spit it out and dropped the entire stick onto the ground. They refused to pay for it. So, the killer said, 'There is a price to be paid for your disrespect.' Just like today in the store! Then, as they are trying to leave, he kills them. He takes the bodies and uses the finger bones for candle wicks.

"Now compare that to what happened at the store today. It was a locally made candle with a really weird wick made by a woman with serious anger issues. And Tom, she gave the exact same threat that was in the story. It was word for word!"

Tom paused. He could see the concern in Julie's eyes.

"The coincidence is a bit freaky, Jewels."

"Right?"

"But I'm sorry. I think it's just a coincidence."

"Nobody ever listens to me," Julie said with frustration.

"Sure we do. Just not when you're talking crazy."

Tom suddenly noticed the room's ceiling was bathed in an orange glow. There was a twinkle of light coming from the other side of the room. He looked over to the nightstand next to his bed. There was a candle burning. But it wasn't just burning. It was crackling.

"Did you light my candle?" Tom asked. He was in shock.

"Yes," Julie said. "Now hear me out."

Tom did not wait for her to continue.

"Jewels! After everything we went through. I can't give that to my mom now!"

"First of all, we are in kind of a life or death situation here. We have no power or heat. Second, you yourself said she probably wouldn't like it because it smells like sesame."

"You're a pain in the ass. I hope you know that."

"Sorry, Tom."

"You can be the one to tell my mom that."

"Trust me, I would love to have a word with her about this stupid candle hunt. Look, Tom, we can get another one another time. Christmas is still a few weeks away. Relax. We have bigger problems right now. Let it go. Enjoy the ride."

Julie turned off the light on her cell phone and placed the phone on the nightstand next to her bed. She slid both arms under the blankets along with her book. For some reason, clutching the book gave her comfort.

Tom frowned and walked over to the candle. He turned off his flashlight and looked straight down into the top of the oddly shaped glass jar with the flip-top lid. The flame from the flat wood wick made an audible crackling sound as it flickered back and forth. A small circle of liquid wax had formed around the wick. The melted wax took on an orange glow. The edges of the glass rim sparkled with tones of white and yellow. Tom held his nose closer to the top and inhaled. The smell of sesame was very mild.

"It's actually a pretty cool candle," Tom said. He tossed his blanket over his bed and began to tuck the corners in.

"Right? I was surprised when it started to crackle like that. Like kindling in a small campfire or something. The flame is really bright, too. Didn't she say it was local?"

Tom spun the candle around to get a better look at the sticker. The wood wick crackled loudly as the hot wax rolled against it. He lifted the lid to get a better look at the sticker.

"FlickerWood Candles," Tom said. He turned to look at Julie, but the chest of drawers between the beds prevented a direct line of sight. He leaned forward so he could see her. She was already buried under her blanket. "Jewels? Did you try searching for FlickerWood Candles on your phone?"

"No! Oh my God, that's brilliant! Hold on."

Julie unlocked her phone and launched the browser. Julie glanced up at the signal-strength indicator: one bar flashed on and off. She waited patiently.

"Well?" Tom asked.

Julie sat up and leaned forward so she could better see Tom.

"It's still loading. I told you there is no signal in this damn gully."

Suddenly, her phone went dark.
"Fuck!" Julie said.
"What?"
"My phone just died."

SIXTEEN

Mother

Despite the freezing temperature, beads of sweat cautiously rolled down Chris' forehead. She had lost track of how long she'd been struggling to loosen her ropes. Her left hand had become useless. The pain in her shoulder had gotten progressively worse, so she had focused on twisting her right wrist repeatedly, while slowly pulling her arm in and out of the knot. She could feel it moving more freely with each passing minute. The rope had also started to flex. She knew it would eventually give way.

Chris looked across the barn at Marc. He was still motionless. Chris was worried that Marc had lost too much blood. *Why won't he wake up?*

"Marc!" Chris cried out.

The Doberman had been lying on its stomach facing Chris. It sat up and growled at her.

"Shut up!" Chris yelled. The dog began to bark. "The first thing I am going to do when I get these ropes off is beat the shit out of you."

Chris turned her attention away from the dog and looked back across the barn.

"Marc! Please wake up!"

He wasn't responding. Chris realized that once free she was going to have to drag Marc all the way out to the truck. With her right foot in so much pain, she wasn't sure how much pressure she could put on it. *Can I even support myself, let alone Marc?*

If she could free at least one of her hands, she could get to her phone in her coat pocket to call for help. *Wait, why haven't Tom or Julie tried to call me?*

Chris was getting light-headed from the blood loss. She took a few deep breaths. She needed to stay calm and regain her focus.

The pig returned through the huge front door, grunting several times as it strolled by Chris. It walked right by Chris, ignoring her, and headed straight to the pot, sniffing its edges. After letting out a few loud snorts, it sauntered back off to the side door behind Chris and exited the barn.

Outside, the wind shifted again and rushed in from the barn's back corner. The stench from the slaughtered cow once more enveloped Chris. She held her breath, and waited until the wind shifted direction again. *Thank God.*

She turned her gaze back to the pot, and then to the far end of the table with the knives. For the first time, she noticed there were saws and axes of various sizes hanging on the walls near the stalls. She turned her eyes back to the metal table in front of her, and the three glass jars nestled at the corner. *Are those candle jars?*

The dog stood up and began to growl again. Chris felt a chill run down her spine. It wasn't from the wind. It was from the thought that had suddenly popped into her head. *Is the legend from that book real? Was Julie right?*

She began to twist her wrist even harder. The skin was becoming raw from the constant grinding against the coarse rope. Her heart raced. As it pounded against her chest, the wound around the arrow in her shoulder throbbed harder and harder. Chris gasped for air as panic set in.

"Don't bother, dear," Mother said.

Chris turned to see the frail old woman standing at the main entrance to the barn. She wore a heavy black sweater that hung to her knees. Her faded blue slippers had been replaced with a pair of thick rubber boots that extended up past her calves and under her nightgown and sweater.

"What the hell is going on, you crazy witch?" Chris screamed.

Mother smiled and walked over to Chris. She stopped a few feet away, next to the Doberman. She held her hand out flat and the dog immediately stopped growling and sat back on its hind legs, silently keeping watch over Chris. Mother rested her hand on the dog's head and gently rubbed his ears.

"Despite her temper, my Sara is an excellent shot," Mother said. "But this storm really tested her skills. Such horrible wind tonight. Truth be told, I'm glad you're awake."

"Why? So you can turn my bones into candlewicks?"

Mother let out a hearty laugh and shook her head back and forth in bemusement.

"You've been reading too many silly stories. Bones can't be used for wicks. They don't burn that way. Although they do make for a nice necklace. Besides, dear, you've seen our candles. You broke plenty of them. Were there any bones in them?"

Chris just stared back, confused by the conversation. Her eyes were heavy. Her shoulder throbbed in pain. Behind her back, out of the old woman's view, she continued to slowly twist and pull her wrist. Chris believed she only needed a few more minutes before her right hand would finally be free. She had to keep her talking.

"So then, what's this all about?" Chris asked.

Mother turned toward the center of the barn with the two large workbenches and huge iron cauldron. She glanced around looking at the walls and stables. There was so much history in this place. So much she wanted to tell her. She walked behind Chris. Chris stopped trying to free herself and made two fists. She could hear the old woman's feet shuffling across the hay-covered floor. Chris looked at the dog. He was watching the old woman now, ignoring Chris. Suddenly, there was a subtle scraping sound. Chris closed her eyes, fearing the worst.

Mother emerged in front of Chris, dragging a small school

chair. She pulled it next to the dog and turned it so that it faced Chris. Chris exhaled a sigh of relief and went back to trying to free her hand.

"I'm getting too old for this," Mother sighed. She sat down in the chair and leaned forward.

Chris sat back as the old woman leaned toward her.

"This home. This barn. They have been in my family for generations. When I married my husband – God rest his soul – he moved in here with the rest of my family. Eventually, the house and farm became ours. We've run a very ... discreet ... candle-making business here on and off for quite a long time. You might even call it a seasonal business. It's been dormant for many years.

"Everything here in this barn has been passed down over the years. Those knives and tools that you see on the table and the walls were all hand-made by my father. Others by my husband. Each one has a purpose. A purpose exists for each to fulfill. We pride ourselves on our use of local ingredients. Why, even the wooden wicks in our candles come from the trees here on this farm."

Mother turned and pointed to the wall over by the stalls.

"You see those axes? Well, those are to chop the trees down. There are some machetes that we then use to cut off the smaller branches. The knives get progressively smaller for the purpose they must serve."

Mother reached into her sweater pocket and pulled out a brown leather sheath and dagger. Chris held her breath, and stopped twisting her wrist. She stared long and hard at the dagger with the bright blue turquoise inlay.

"This here," Mother continued, "is how we do the fine detailing." She pulled the dagger from the sheath and held it flat across her palm. She then waved it in front of Chris. "Those wicks are hand cut to an exact standard."

Mother stopped waving the dagger and pointed it at Chris.

"We take pride in our work," Mother said. She slowly returned the knife to its sheath and put it back in her pocket.

Chris finally exhaled.

"But what makes our candles special isn't the wicks, even if that's the most intricate work that we have to do. No, dear.

What makes them special is the tallow. Do you know what tallow is, dear?"

Chris stared at her with a blank face. Mother sighed.

"Tallow is simply rendered fat. It's a matter of boiling the fat down to convert it to tallow. Not all fats are the same. Some will get too soft. When making candlewax, you need a fat that will stay firm when it cools. And you simply must avoid getting any of the organ meat mixed in or you will have a nasty-smelling candle."

Mother paused, looking Chris up and down.

"I'm sure you know how important it is for a candle to have a nice scent," Mother said.

Chris continued to glare at her, refusing to give her the satisfaction of a reaction.

"At one time, we had many animals on this farm. Horses, goats, pigs. Cows, of course. The property extends very far back. Very far. The goats and pigs were our main source of income. We would use them for milk, cheese, food, and tallow. Our tallow makes all of the difference."

Chris nodded as if she was following along, but it was just to distract her and to keep the conversation going. Her focus was on her wrist. The rope continued to loosen. She figured she would just need the old woman close enough to be able to pull the dagger from her pocket. She would be easy to knock down with only one hand free.

"Traditionally, tallow comes from the fat that's around a cow's kidneys," Mother said. "But our family's candle recipe was primarily goat fat. If we didn't have enough goat fat, we would blend it with the cow fat. Or whatever source we could find. But pure goat fat was always preferred.

"And we would use all of the fat we could extract. 'Waste not, want not,' as my husband used to say. God rest his soul. It's important to use as much of the beast as you can. We used to make soaps with the tallow as well. And the flesh and organs have so many uses. Our neighbor Bobby over in Truro used to make a fine sausage with some of our supplies. We were in business together for quite some time. But that's another story."

Mother stood up from the chair. She put a hand to her back

as she got up and leaned forward to stretch. The cold weather made her already stiff joints ache even more. She looked around the barn. The pig came strolling in again. Mother walked up to it and gently ran her hand across its coarse skin.

"Pigs make great sausage. Goats make great candles. And as you can see, Miss Becker, we are all out of goats."

Mother smacked the pig on its backside. It ran off to the back corner of the barn. She followed it around to the other side of the table and then stopped in front of the cauldron. The light from the flames of the fire pit flickered and danced across her creased neck and chin. She reached over to the table next to the steaming pot and picked up a two-foot-long ladle that had been lying next to the knives. She lowered it into the cauldron and began to stir. She leaned over the pot. Inhaled. And then smiled.

"Nobody will be coming to rescue you," Mother said. She held the huge spoon up to her nose as if she were about to take a sip. Instead, she just took another deep breath. "My daughter is taking care of your truck right now. It will be buried by morning. Oh, and all of your phones and little gizmos that were in that bag have all been destroyed."

Chris stared back in shock. Her heart was pounding hard in her chest. She continued to twist her wrist faster and faster.

"My friend that made the sausages used to have a saying," Mother continued. "We can't have any loose ends."

Mother chuckled at her own joke. She then put the ladle back down on the bench next to one of the turquoise inlaid knives. She smiled and started to walk toward Marc.

"Why are you doing this?" Chris screamed. "Why?"

The dog leaped up onto all fours and snarled. Chris began to yank both of her wrists hard now. The pain in her shoulder was excruciating, but she knew she was running out of time. The old woman was on the other side of the barn now. Chris tried desperately to break free.

"Well, you broke all of our candles at the store today. We need new ones, dear."

Mother stood beside Marc and ran her right hand over his head. She grabbed him by the chin and turned his face up toward hers. His body remained motionless.

"You're insane!" Chris yelled out.

"Sara told me he was the nice one in the group. And he was kind enough to pay for the broken candles, too. Pity."

Mother let go of Marc's chin. His head slumped over. She walked over to the two bodies that were tied to the post several feet past Marc. A frown formed as she looked down at the young Asian couple.

"Such a waste," Mother sighed.

She walked behind them and inspected the tarp. There were three hooks holding it in place. She unlatched them and the top half of the tarp fell forward. Chris turned away in disgust at what was underneath. Both bodies were naked. Ropes cut across their chests and around the main beam, holding them upright. Their arms were missing. Mother walked around front and grabbed the tarp and turned toward Marc. As she walked past him, the tarp covering the young couple pulled away, revealing their bodies in full. Their legs had been cut off. Both torsos had been sliced open and gutted. They were completely mutilated.

As Mother reached the end of the table, one of the hooks from the tarp she was dragging caught the end of the tarp covering Marc. Chris looked on in repulsion as the tarp slowly rolled off of Marc and fell to the ground. Marc's legs were gone. Chris shook her head and tried to focus, wondering if her eyes were playing tricks on her. They weren't. Marc's legs had been cut off halfway above his knees. The school chair he was in was soaked in blood. *In Marc's blood*, Chris realized.

"Marc!" Chris cried out. She couldn't believe what she was seeing. *His legs are gone!*

Chris was in a full panic, gasping for air as she tried to keep from sobbing. She pulled furiously at the ropes around her wrists. As she did, the realization of what had happened rose deep from within her gut. *Marc is dead!*

Chris began to cry. The tears burned as they ran down her face. The ice-cold temperatures crystalized them as they fell from her cheeks. Guilt suddenly washed over her. Her head filled with the memories of so many arguments and disagreements. She thought back to their last fight at the truck earlier this evening. *If only I had listened.*

Mother paid no attention to Chris. She had not meant to pull the tarp off Marc. She went back and separated the two tarps, leaving the blood-soaked tarp in a heap on the ground. Marc's severed corpse sat exposed. Blood dripped from the edges of the old wooden school chair, falling onto the hay scattered on the barn floor. Mother grabbed the other tarp that had been covering the Asian couple and continued around the table.

"You two eat much too healthy," Mother said. "That one is too lean. I'll definitely have to use some extra cow tallow for this next batch of candles. I can't use my last cow. Sara was so upset that I had to kill Anna. I don't know what she'd do if we had to sacrifice Daisy as well. Times like these ..."

Mother turned and looked at the stalls at the back of the barn. Daisy stared back in silence.

"I'm glad to see you have some curves on you," Mother continued. "There should be some good fat in there that we can use. Maybe I'll reach out to Bobby to see if he wants the leftovers."

The dog was still barking at Chris. As Mother walked by him, she put her hand out flat and he stopped. She walked up to Chris and dropped both tarps near her feet.

Up close, Chris could see that the tarp that had been covering the couple was caked in dried frozen blood. Mother used her rubber boots to kick the tarp out around Chris' chair. She continued to yank at her ropes. She no longer cared if the old woman could see that she was trying to escape. The pocket with the dagger was less than a foot from Chris. The heavy knit sweater swung back and forth from the weight of the knife that was nestled inside. The edge of the turquoise inlaid handle poked out from the top of the pocket. It was so close to Chris. *So close.*

"There," Mother said with a smile. She stepped back to inspect how well she had spread out the tarps. "That should do."

Chris pulled harder and harder. She looked across the barn at Marc's body. *It's just me now.* Her right wrist was finally twisting freely. She squeezed her fingers together to make her hand as narrow as possible. It was almost through the rope.

Mother walked over to the table on the far side of the cauldron. After a short inspection of her options, she picked up a saw. The blade was eighteen inches long with a jagged-tooth design. The metal was heavily worn down. The handle had the same turquoise inlay and nickel spacer as the dagger in her pocket. She walked back over to Chris.

Chris was now shaking and pulling her arms violently. She began to scream and cry from the pain in her shoulder and foot as she used all her strength to try to break free. Tears continued to stream down her face. Mother raised the saw in front of Chris. She stopped moving and stared at the blade. The teeth were stained black and covered in bits of fabric, flesh, and bone. The wind outside howled as a huge gust blew through the barn. The stench from the dead bodies in the barn washed over her. She glanced over at the cauldron, realizing for the first time that it was most likely Marc's legs that were boiling away inside. Chris tried to catch her breath. Mother lowered the saw and rested the blade across Chris' legs. The jagged teeth pressed ever so slightly against her jeans. They were ready to be fed.

"You will both make a fine set of candles," Mother said. "And don't worry, dear. I'll make sure they are scented."

Chris cried out in agony as Mother thrust the blade deep into her right thigh.

SEVENTEEN

Seabreeze

It was midnight, and the snow was still falling heavily across the outer tip of Cape Cod. Power had yet to be restored anywhere in Provincetown. At the bottom of the entrance to Seabreeze Village, the wind howled as it whipped through the branches of the huge American Holly tree. All twelve townhomes sat in complete darkness, save for one upstairs window in Unit #1. The dim orange glow from the FlickerWood candle in the guest bedroom danced across the bathroom window.

Inside the guest bedroom, Julie was fast asleep, wearing her winter coat, gloves, and the multi-colored hat her ya-ya had knit for her. The Zombunnies were keeping her feet warm, along with three layers of socks and two sets of pajamas. She had the blanket pulled all the way over her head.

The FlickerWood candle was still on the nightstand between Tom's bed and the bathroom. The top of the wick crackled softly. The sound and light were not as intense as it had been earlier. The candle had been burning for many hours, and the top layer had completely liquefied. Tom was buried under his blanket, curled up in a ball and hugging a pillow. His thick sleeping mask sheltered his eyes from the light from the candle.

The window next to Julie's bed was covered in beads of ice and snow. Fifteen feet below was the back patio, with the table, chairs, and candle that Chris had packed for Marc. Everything was covered in several inches of snow.

In the darkness of the backyard, a gloved hand cleared some of the snow off the table and tilted the metal citronella candle. There was the key. *Under the candle,* Sara said to herself.

She took the key and walked over to the French door at the back of the patio. The key slid in with little effort. After undoing the deadbolt, she tried the main lock. She smiled. Sara tossed the key back onto the wrought iron table and then quietly entered the condo.

The downstairs was pitch black, but her eyes adjusted quickly. Everything was silent. She turned on her flashlight and swept the beam across the rooms. Although the temperature in the condo had dropped to sixty degrees, it was still much warmer than outside. The snow and ice that covered Sara's hat, coat, and boots quickly began to melt.

When she had walked down the driveway earlier, she had noticed the faint light coming from the upstairs window. She made her way over to the staircase, turned off her flashlight, and started her ascent. The townhouse was new and very well-constructed. The stairs barely made a sound as she worked her way to the second floor.

Sara paused halfway up the stairs to rest. Her right leg throbbed with pain. She ran her hand over her wound, and took a moment to catch her breath. As she approached the top of the stairs, Sara could see light coming from the first door. She stepped inside and looked around the room. There were two beds. Each was occupied. *Perfect,* Sara thought.

She glanced over at the candle burning in the corner. The crackling wick and scent of sesame made her smile. *I'll have to take that back to Mother.*

Sara removed the glove from her right hand and placed it in her coat pocket. She reached into her other pocket and pulled out a leather sheath and dagger. The dagger was the same one she had used on the last batch of wicks. The blade was duller than she would have preferred, but it would serve its purpose.

She pulled the dagger from the sheath. The light from the FlickerWood candle reflected off the blade as she changed her grip on the turquoise and nickel inlaid handle. Sara walked around to the side of the bed next to the window. She ran her eyes up and down the lump under the blanket before settling on a target point. She raised her right arm and quickly thrust it down into the middle of the bed, then yanked it back up.

"Oh my God!" Julie screamed. Julie flung off her blanket. She was holding the book of urban legends in her left hand. It had a huge gash in it from the dagger. She looked up in total shock. "Tom! Tom!"

Sara paused momentarily, confused as to why this girl wasn't injured. She lashed out again with the dagger. Julie held her arm up to block her, and the blade again went into the book, this time getting lodged in the edge of the binding. Sara yanked the knife back and tore the book out of Julie's hand.

Tom sat up and ripped his eye mask off. He heard Julie crying. The flashlight was next to the candle on the nightstand. He flicked it on and aimed it at the other end of the room. He was stunned to see the woman from the candle store. *What is she doing here?*

At that moment, Tom noticed the book in her hand with the knife sticking out of it. His heart began to race. The powerful beam cut across the room, shining directly into Sara's face. She tossed both hands up to block the light.

"She's trying to kill me!" Julie screamed.

Tom looked around the room in a panic. He felt the blood rush to his face as he crawled to the middle of his bed. His heart pounded harder and harder, beating like a tribal drum. Every blood vessel in his body seemed to pulse and pound at the same time. He looked at the doorway that led to the hall. He could hear his father's voice echoing in his head.

Run!

Tom dropped the flashlight onto his bed, and stared at the exit.

Sara finally managed to pull the dagger from the book. She slid the book into her pocket. Julie was completely frozen in terror and unable to move.

"I need to take both of you back to the barn to join your friends," Sara said. "Mother is waiting. There are candles to be made. Time to pay."

"Tom!" Julie screamed again.

Tom looked at Julie and the woman standing over him. He saw his dad, lying on the kitchen table. The backlit figure standing over him, brandishing a knife.

"No!" Tom roared.

Tom turned and looked back at the candle. The tip of the wick was red and crackling. The top inch of the jar was filled with wax that had been simmering at over one-hundred-thirty degrees for hours. He looked at the heavy metal flashlight lying on the bed. The beam was now pointed at the doorway. Adrenaline coursed throughout his body. Tom knew what he had to do.

He picked up the flashlight and aimed it directly at Sara's face. The LEDs burned into her eyes, momentarily blinding her. She turned her head to the side and tossed her right hand up to block the beam. She took a moment to switch the dagger to her left hand. Tom dropped the flashlight and lunged for the candle. He flipped the hinged lid shut. The flame immediately went out. He grabbed the glass jar, turned his body, and threw it, lid-first, across the room at Sara.

Sara's vision was filled with white spots from the beam of the flashlight. She didn't see the candle until it was right in front of her. She instinctively reached out to catch it with both hands.

As she caught the candle, the lid flipped open, sending hot wax straight at her face. She screamed in agony as the searing hot tallow melted into her skin. She took a few steps back in shock. As she did, she caught her foot on Julie's duffle bag in the alcove in front of the window. Her right leg wobbled as she attempted to keep herself from losing her balance.

Fight or flight, Tom thought. He reached for the heavy metal flashlight resting on his bed. In his panic he fumbled, knocking it to the ground. It rolled across the floor, coming to a rest against the wall opposite his bed.

"Fuck!" Tom yelled.

Sara was still in shock from the burning candlewax and couldn't open her right eye. She turned to Tom and stared at him.

"Mother will make you pay!" Sara cried.

Tom leaped from his bed and snatched the flashlight off the floor, aiming the powerful light directly at Sara's face. He kept the beam focused on her as he charged past the end of Julie's bed.

Sara was completely blinded. The full 3,000 lumens burned into her one open eye. She held the candle jar up to shield her face from the light.

Tom leaned forward and ran full speed into Sara, keeping the light aimed directly at her head. Her arms were raised, exposing her torso. His left shoulder plunged deep into her stomach. Sara gasped as the air was thrust from her lungs. Her injured right leg immediately buckled as her left leg fell backward over Julie's duffle bag.

Tom fell to the floor and looked up to see Sara crash through the giant arched window. The sound of the shattering glass rattled Julie from her comatose state. The wind howled as it roared into the bedroom.

Sara clutched her family candle and dagger as she flew out into the cold darkness of the night. The right side of her face was covered in wax. Wind shot across her skin, instantly hardening the sesame-scented tallow. She screamed in terror as she plunged to the ground.

Tom rose to his feet and looked at the shattered window. Shards of jagged glass jutted out along the edges of the window frame. The wind shrieked as it blasted snow into the bedroom. He turned to Julie. She was sobbing uncontrollably on the bed. He sat next to her and took her by the hands, squeezing her purple leather gloves.

"Are you OK, Jewels? Did she hurt you?"

"Oh my God, Tom. What the hell?"

Tom pulled her close. Julie began to cry heavily onto his shoulder.

"It's OK," Tom said. "We're OK now."

"Wait," Julie said. "Where is she?"

She pulled away and looked up at Tom.

"Is she still out there? Are we safe?"

Tom jumped up and grabbed the flashlight off the floor. It had survived the fall. Julie slowly approached the broken window. She pulled her knit hat down tighter the closer she got to it. The bitterly cold wind and snow cut across her face. Tom put his arm around her. Together they stepped over her duffle bag and leaned out the window.

Down below was nothing but snow. Tom aimed the powerful LEDs out the window and swept the beam across the backyard. The light from the flashlight danced off of the pieces of broken glass scattered across the ground. There was a large indentation in the snow just beyond the patio. Footsteps led away from the impact area and disappeared around the corner.

Suddenly, they heard an engine struggling to turn over. It cranked a few times and choked and stuttered before finally coming to life. Looking out the broken window, Tom and Julie could only see the car's taillights in the distance as it pulled away. Tom aimed the flashlight at the vehicle. He immediately recognized the old Jeep Cherokee from the candle store.

"She's gone, Jewels," Tom said.

"Are you sure?" Julie asked, wiping the tears from her face. She had finally stopped crying.

"We better double-check. In case she wasn't alone. But that was definitely her Jeep."

They headed downstairs, letting the flashlight be their guide. The steps were wet from Sara's boots. Tom could feel his socks getting moist with each step. He held the flashlight out in front of him, like a saber. Julie stayed close behind with her gloved hands on his shoulders. They stopped at the bottom of the stairs.

Tom focused the light on the front door. He could tell it was locked, even the deadbolt. Then he swept the beam over to the side door. It was also locked and bolted. He walked over to the living room and looked at the French door that led to the back patio. The door was closed but unlocked.

"This is where she came in," Tom said. He reached for the

doorknob.

"Wait!" Julie yelled.

She ran to the kitchen and rummaged through the drawers. She returned to Tom's side holding an eight-inch carving knife. Her hands were trembling.

Tom opened the door cautiously and looked around, sweeping the flashlight's beam back and forth across the yard. He noticed a flicker of gold on the patio table. The citronella candle had been turned over.

Tom stepped outside and grabbed the key from the table. He aimed the flashlight around the side of the yard toward the top of the hill. Julie stayed huddled inside at the edge of the doorway, clutching the knife.

"She's gone, Jewels."

Tom went back inside, closed the door, and locked it.

"Are you sure?"

"Trust me. How are you? Are you hurt?"

"I'm OK. I think."

Tom used the flashlight to check Julie up and down. He noticed the left sleeve on her jacket was slightly torn and stained with small drops of blood.

"Shit!" Julie said as Tom pointed to it.

Julie pulled off her bulky jacket and rolled up the sleeves of her pajamas. A small cut ran a few inches across the inside of her arm. It wasn't deep.

"That stings," Julie said.

"Good thing you were wearing eighty layers of clothes."

"It was that book. That stupid fucking urban legends book stopped most of that knife."

Julie looked around the condo, trying to gather her thoughts.

"Tom, how the fuck did she get in here?"

Tom opened the palm of his hand and showed Julie the key.

"The candle outside. It was knocked over. My guess is she used the key that was under it."

"But how ..." Julie stopped as she remembered laughing with Chris about needing a new candle to hide the key. They had repeatedly joked about it at the store. "Fuck!"

Tom walked over to the sectional and sat down. He placed

the flashlight on its base and aimed it straight up at the ceiling to better illuminate the room. Julie sat by his side and pulled her purple gloves off and tossed them on the coffee table.

"How did she find us?" Julie asked.

"I don't know, Jewels."

Julie placed the kitchen knife down on the table and clasped her hands together. She couldn't stop shaking.

"Something must have happened when they went to get the backpack," Tom said. "She said she ... she had them. Didn't she?"

A cold breeze cut across the room. It had spun its way down the staircase, from the shattered window in the upstairs bedroom.

"I told you earlier, Tom. I said I had a bad feeling about that woman. You still think I'm crazy for thinking this is tied to the legend?"

"Jewels ..."

"Tom, I think ..." Julie paused. She felt her throat close up as she struggled to get the words out. "I think Marc and Chris are dead."

"Don't say that! We need to focus! We can start with the cops."

"We don't have a phone."

"The police station is not that far from us. I think it's like a ten-minute walk over to Shank Painter Road. It could take a bit longer in this storm. They can patch you up. And maybe even take us to the store."

"The store? The one in Truro?"

"Yes. We have to start somewhere. We have to find that woman."

EIGHTEEN

Legendary

It was just after 1:30 a.m. when the Ford Police Interceptor finally clawed its way onto Route 6 West. The main highway was in much better condition than the side roads. The state had been doing an excellent job of running plows to keep it somewhat clear. Officer Trevor Stevens of the Provincetown Police Department kept his speed pegged at a cautious 30 mph.

"I still can't believe I let you two talk me into this," Stevens said with frustration. He glanced over at his rearview mirror and let his eyes rest on the two petite occupants sitting in the back seat.

"It's the right thing to do," Tom said.

"We really appreciate it," Julie added.

"I appreciate your appreciation, Miss Perez," Stevens said. "But I'm not doing this out of kindness. It was the only way to shut the other one up."

"Julie. You can call me Julie. So how long ..."

"This was the only logical choice," Tom interjected. "You searched the townhouse. All you found was a broken window scattered across the backyard. Other than some faded tracks

182

there was nothing else. Going to the store in Truro is the only way we can find that woman and try to save Marc and Chris!"

Julie reached over and grabbed Tom by the hand. She feared his cavalier attitude was pushing the limits of Officer Stevens' patience. Tom yanked his hand away and stared out the window.

"How's your arm?" Stevens asked.

"It's fine," Julie replied. "Thanks for patching me up."

"Will the Truro police be meeting us at the store?" Tom asked.

"How could they?" Stevens replied. "You have no address for me. No name. No number. I'll call them when we find it."

At thirty-four years old and with no family, Officer Stevens had volunteered to work the main desk during the blizzard. His quiet night in the station had turned into something completely unexpected.

Tom's gaze remained locked on the world unfolding outside of the vehicle. He squinted as he tried to see through the snow rushing past the window. The buildings, trees, and side roads were a jumbled blur. The images, however, were becoming familiar to him.

"I think we're getting close," Tom said.

The pulsating rhythm of the blue and red police lights danced off the falling snow as Officer Stevens slowed to 20 mph. Tom pressed his face up against the glass to get a better look. Slowly, out of the darkness, he could see the outline of the small store they had visited earlier.

"There! There!" Tom said. "The little brown house set back under the trees."

Officer Stevens turned into the parking lot. The building did not look at all familiar to him, despite endless drives up and down Route 6. The dark brown paint color, small size, and setting under the trees made it all but invisible.

The snow depth in the lot varied from six inches to almost two feet. The wind from the blizzard had blown most of it toward the far end of the lot. It had not been cleared, and was a pristine blanket of white snowdrifts. The Interceptor could only get about halfway into the lot before the snow got too deep. Officer Stevens parked at an angle so that the lights from the vehicle flooded the front of the building.

"Wait here," Stevens said.

"No," Tom replied. He was quite stern. "Take us with you."

"Please," Julie added. "We can show you everything that happened inside."

The officer stepped out of the SUV, closed the door, and turned on his flashlight. Standing just over six feet tall, Officer Stevens cut an imposing figure. He pulled his hat down tight over his shaved head. The snow melted as it landed on his warm dark skin. The first thing he noticed was the lack of tire tracks. There was no indication that any vehicle had recently been in front of the store. It looked like the place had been deserted since before the heavy snowfall began. After a brief scan of the area, he let Tom and Julie out of the back of the SUV. They headed toward the covered entrance to the store.

Once they got to the porch, the policeman aimed his flashlight through the window of the candle store. Tom and Julie pressed their faces to the glass and tried to follow the beam of light as it shot back and forth across the interior. The light went off.

"Hold on," Stevens said. "I'm going back to my vehicle to call this in. Stay here."

Tom and Julie looked out across the lot. With the bright lights from the police SUV illuminating the area, they could see just how powerful the blizzard had been. Route 6 was fairly clear, but there were a few small pine trees down on the side of the store, and along the main road.

"Do you think the local police will help?" Julie asked Tom.

"I hope so."

Julie turned back to the store and pressed her face against the window. She was trying to get a good look at the front counter that had been smashed.

"Tom, where's that flashlight you had?"

Tom searched his pockets.

"Shit, Jewels. I left it back at the condo."

Officer Stevens opened his door and stepped out of the SUV. He motioned for Tom and Julie to come back over to him.

"Get in," Stevens yelled. "It will be warmer in here, and

we've got a bit of a wait."

Once Tom and Julie were safely inside the vehicle, Officer Stevens turned up the heat.

"I talked to an officer here in Truro," Stevens said. "He didn't completely understand what I was telling him. Probably because I am just as confused. This place looks deserted. I don't know what you expect to find inside."

"Evidence," Tom said.

Officer Stevens managed a small grin at the young man's determination.

"I gave him our location. Relax and enjoy the heat. He's on his way."

***

It was roughly ten minutes later when a flashing blue and red glow began reflecting off of the snowdrifts and trees across Route 6. Seconds later a Dodge Charger Pursuit car appeared from around the bend and pulled into the parking lot. The car stopped several feet away from the Interceptor.

Officer Jones emerged from his vehicle and studied the small store shrouded beneath the snow-covered pine trees. He glanced over at the big Ford SUV and nodded.

Officer Stevens opened his door and waved toward the young policeman. Officer Jones motioned toward the store's porch. As he stepped away from his vehicle a strong gust of wind whipped the door from his hand, slamming it shut. He shrugged it off, and headed toward the store. Officer Stevens, Julie, and Tom followed him there.

Once under the overhang, the young cop from Truro removed his hat and used it to dust the snow from his shoulders and sleeves. He shook his head in frustration.

"Officer Stevens?" Officer Jones asked. "Officer Jones. We spoke earlier. I'm hoping you can clear up exactly why you dragged me out in this storm. We've got a skeleton crew running tonight. Power outages all over the place. It's all kind of crazy."

"This isn't the quiet night I had hoped for either," Officer Stevens replied. "Let me tell you what I know. It was around

12:40 a.m. when these two came into my station. They claimed a woman had entered the townhouse where they were staying. She attacked this woman, Julie, with a knife. This young man, Tom, fought back and knocked the assailant down. She fell through a second story window, but managed to get away."

"And tell me again how Truro fits into this. You weren't clear when you called this in."

"We met the woman at this store," Tom said. "I think she owned it. Anyway, there was an accident in the store and a bunch of stuff got broken. She freaked out at us."

"She threatened us," Julie added.

"In the rush to leave, I left my knapsack here," Tom continued. "Two of our friends came back to get my bag. That was last night around 5 p.m."

"When the woman attacked me at the condo, she said she was going to take us back to be with our friends," Julie added. "We think she is holding them captive. Or that ... that they may already be dead."

Why does Julie keep saying that? Tom wondered. He wasn't ready to accept it. He closed his eyes, trying to recall everything the woman had said, but one phrase kept playing in his mind, over and over. *There are candles to be made.*

Officer Jones paused for several seconds as he studied the faces of the three strangers who had brought him out on this stormy evening.

"This store here?" Jones asked as he nodded toward the front door.

"Yes, Officer," Julie said.

"Interesting. Officer Stevens, can you join me? You two stay here."

Officer Jones led Officer Stevens back out into the lot, and the two trudged through the snow and headed around to the back of the building.

"Do you really think we'll find anything inside?" Julie asked. "That old Jeep seems long gone."

"If my backpack is there it means they never even got this far," Tom said.

"Maybe," Julie said.

Behind the rear of the building, Officer Jones approached

the entrance to the candle store with caution. The back door was partially open. Snow had drifted inside. There were no tracks in the snow. He pushed the door open the rest of the way and took a moment to inspect the handle and lock on the door.

"Interesting," Jones said.

"What is?" Stevens asked.

"I was out here two weeks ago just before Thanksgiving. The owners had reported a break-in. They were pretty upset. I recommended a great locksmith to fix this door. They were planning to close up for the season the weekend after the holiday. They said they were going to get it fixed right away. So why is this lock still broken?"

The two entered the back office and stock room. It was a small space with numerous shelves, a metal desk, and a washroom. Everything seemed fine. They stepped into the main store. Officer Stevens could see Tom and Julie looking inside through the front window. The blue and red flashing lights from the two police vehicles created a surreal strobe effect inside the building. They walked around for a couple of minutes with their flashlights, but it was apparent nobody else was in the store. Officer Jones approached the main counter and noticed the shattered glass top.

"This wasn't here two weeks ago," Jones said.

Officer Stevens studied the display case. It didn't look like it had been ransacked, just shattered. He walked to the front door and let Tom and Julie inside.

"Thanks," Julie said as she entered the store. "It's freezing out there!"

Tom removed his gloves and looked around the store. He immediately walked over to the main counter where he had left his backpack.

"It's not here."

"What?" Stevens asked.

"My backpack. The whole reason our friends came back here to get it. I left it right here next to this counter."

"So does that mean they took it and left, or did the owner take it before they got here?" Julie asked.

Tom shook his head in confusion as he looked around the

store. Julie glanced back at the giant wall of unscented candles. She looked up at the sign above the display and thought of Chris.

"Wait, where is it?" Tom asked. He pointed to a large empty space at the center of the store.

"It's gone!" Julie said.

"What is?" Jones asked.

"The table that got knocked over," Tom said.

"Back it up, Tom," Stevens said. "Tell us what happened here."

Tom walked over to the middle of the store where the candle display had been set up. He turned and looked around, searching for shards of glass from the shattered candles. He didn't see any, but it was hard to see anything with the flashing blue and red lights.

"So, there was a small table right about here," Tom said, pointing to the floor. "It had about a dozen candles on it. Our friend Chris accidentally knocked the table over. Almost all of the candle jars broke. The woman freaked out."

"The woman?" Jones asked. "The owner?"

"Yes," Tom said. "She never told us her name."

"You said this was yesterday?" Jones asked.

"Yes."

"That can't be right. They closed a week ago."

"No," Julie said. "I heard her say she was closing up for the season that afternoon, which was yesterday."

"This doesn't add up," Jones said. His tone was a mix of frustration and confusion. He turned to Officer Stevens. "Why would they close shop a week later than planned and still not fix that back door?"

"What about the back door?" Julie asked.

"Something's off," Stevens said, ignoring Julie. "Go on Tom."

"I had already bought a candle from her. We tried to make things right after Chris broke everything, but she just freaked out. She screamed at us to leave, and when we hesitated, she smashed that countertop."

"She also said we would pay for what we had done," Julie added. "That's why she came to the townhouse. To kill us."

"You're telling me the woman that owns this store is a killer?" Jones asked. "Over some broken candles?"

"Attempted killer," Tom said.

"Officer Jones, have you heard of FlickerWood Candles?" Julie asked.

"No."

"That's what Tom bought, and what we broke. I think the woman might even make the candles."

"I met the owners," Jones said. "They bought this place earlier this year. They never told me anything about them being in the candle-making business. And they most definitely are not killers."

Julie walked over to the main counter and looked inside the case at the broken shards of glass.

"Tom. The books!" Julie said. "They're gone."

Tom walked over to the counter next to Julie.

"That's weird," Tom said. "My pack, the candles, the table, and the books."

"It's like ... like they were never here," Julie said.

Officer Jones had had enough. He looked at his watch. It was already after 2 a.m.

"OK, let me see if I can sum this up," Jones said. "You two come into this store that to my knowledge closed a week ago. Your friend breaks some stuff. The woman screams and breaks that counter. She makes some threats. You run out leaving your backpack behind. Your friends come back here to get it, and you never hear from them again. Then a couple of hours ago, that same woman attacked you in your condo and tried to kill you. But she fell out some window and escaped."

"Yes, Officer, that pretty much sums it up," Tom said.

Officer Jones frowned. He looked at Tom and Julie briefly and then turned to face Officer Stevens.

"All right, so this is what I'm going to do," Jones said. "I'm going to note this broken glass countertop as well as the back door still being busted from the other week." He turned and looked over at Tom and Julie. "But I think you two need to go back to Provincetown with Officer Stevens. There really isn't much we can do here."

"But ..." Tom said.

"I agree," Stevens said, as he cut Tom off.

Officer Stevens opened the front door and walked out onto the covered porch with Tom and Julie. Officer Jones locked the door from the inside and went back through the office to try to secure the busted rear entrance.

"I'm sorry," Stevens said. "I know you both hoped to find more answers here."

"It's OK," Julie said. "Thanks for trying. We knew it was a long-shot."

Tom walked over to the edge of the porch and stared out at Route 6. The snow had finally stopped falling. The wind had quieted down. Julie joined him and put her arm around him.

"It's a dead end," Tom said.

"Not at all," Stevens said. "Officer Jones already filed a report on this place. He met the owners. If everything you say is true then ..."

"Oh my God!" Julie said. "He can take us there!"

Officer Jones came around the corner and joined them on the porch.

"Are we all set here?" Jones asked.

"The owner!" Julie said. "You said you met her."

"Yes. I met both owners."

"Do you know where they live?" Tom asked. His voice rose in excitement over this latest development.

"Yes. I have that info from the report they filed two weeks ago."

Tom and Julie smiled.

"Then you can take us there!" Tom asked. "That's where Marc and Chris will be! Can we go to their house?"

"House?" Jones replied. "No, they have a small cottage out on Drummer Cove. They just moved here earlier this year from Boston."

"She lives there with her mom, right?" Julie asked.

"Her mom?" Jones replied.

"She said that Marc and Chris were with her mother," Tom added. "Is that the other owner?"

Officer Jones shook his head and sighed.

"What did she look like?" Jones asked. "The woman from this store that attacked you earlier."

"Probably mid-forties," Tom said. "A few inches taller than Julie. Very stocky build. Long, wavy brown hair."

"That sounds about right," Julie added.

"Caucasian?" Jones asked.

"Well, yes ..." Tom replied.

"OK," Jones said. "We're done here. Officer Stevens, I'll be in touch."

Officer Jones stepped off the porch and headed back toward the Dodge Charger Pursuit. Tom and Julie stared at each other confused and a bit surprised at his abrupt exit. The officer stopped halfway through the lot, and turned back to the three of them.

"This store is owned by a young married couple. Early twenties. Asian."

***

Tom and Julie sat in silence in the back of the police SUV. The tires roared as they rolled over Route 6 East, heading back to Provincetown. Officer Stevens had already made some calls trying to find a place that they could stay for the night. The town was still without power, but he had managed to find a place that had working fireplaces. The owner was more than happy to take them in for the evening.

"Thanks again for everything, Officer Stevens," Julie said.

"Trevor," Stevens said. "You can call me Trevor. I'm sorry things didn't pan out at that candle store. My guess is that whoever broke in there two weeks ago had come back to finish what they had started. And that's the woman you ran into yesterday. I'll be working with Officer Jones and the rest of the Truro and Provincetown police to get this resolved for you two. If there was a break-in at the store, they may have fingerprints and other evidence we can use. We also have to do a full investigation at the townhouse. It may take some time, though."

"We understand," Julie said.

Officer Stevens looked up into his rearview mirror and adjusted it so that he could see Tom in the back seat. He had not said a word since they left the store. His hands were folded in his lap and he had tears running down his cheeks.

"How are you doing, Tom?" Stevens asked.

Tom looked up, but did not answer him.

"You've both had a traumatic experience," Stevens continued. "There are probably things that have slipped your mind. That's common. I guarantee you that over the next few days and weeks you will remember more. It will take time."

Tom turned and looked at Julie.

"This is all my fault, Jewels. All of it."

"Don't say that, Tom," Julie said.

"If I hadn't left my pack there. If I hadn't been so obsessed with finding that stupid perfect gift! None of this would have happened. I own this. It's on me."

"Listen to me. Hey!" Julie grabbed Tom by his chin and locked eyes with him. "Nobody is to blame for this, OK? Marc is the one that wanted to go to Wellfleet in the first place. I am the one that shoved Chris. Chris is the one that knocked the table over. You know who's to blame?"

"Who?" Tom asked.

"That fucking psycho bitch that tried to kill us!"

Tom shook his head. He pulled away from her and turned to look out the window. They were passing the Days Cottages. The small buildings, normally so cheerful, were blanketed in snow and ice. He closed his eyes and thought back to the attack in the condo. *There are candles to be made.*

Tom opened his eyes, suddenly recalling what she said next. *Time to pay.*

"Time to pay," Tom said aloud. "Jewels, what if … if … what if you're right? That we are never going to see Marc and Chris again."

"You can't give up hope," Stevens said. He had been listening intently from the front seat.

"We have nothing to go on," Tom said. He leaned forward toward Officer Stevens. "All we have is a description. We don't know her name, or the license plate on her Jeep, or even where she lives. Nothing!"

"It's a start," Stevens said.

"Tom is right," Julie said. Her voice quivered as she thought back to the attack in the bedroom. "She was trying to kill me.

You didn't hear what she said to us. I just … I just don't see how they could still be alive."

Julie paused briefly to compose herself.

"She had this look in her eyes," she continued. "Marc and Chris were already dead. Tom and I were going to be next. She was there to finish the job. That's what I felt at the time. It's what I still believe."

"Look," Stevens said. "These things take time. It's possible that your friends just got stuck somewhere in this blizzard."

"No," Julie said.

Officer Stevens realized he was not going to win this argument. He was going to have to let the two of them work through it on their own time.

The Interceptor crossed over the Provincetown line. Julie looked out her window at the "Welcome to Provincetown" sign. The entire sign was covered in snow and ice, making it unreadable. She turned and looked at Tom.

"It's the legend," she said.

"Jewels …"

"What legend?" Stevens asked.

"It was in that book I used to block the attack," Julie explained. "I read this story on our drive out here from Providence on Friday. It was an urban legend about a candlemaker. He would use the bones of his victims as the wicks in the candles that he made. It was an act of vengeance against those that showed disrespect. We all laughed about it. The woman in the candle store had copies of that same book sitting on the counter. I asked her about that legend. She said it was only partially true. She seemed to know more than she was telling us. Her threat to us was an almost exact quote from the story. It was practically word for word. She said we would all 'pay the price.'"

NINETEEN

Providence

Tom sat with Max on the floor of his living room, his back propped up against the couch. Max's front legs were sprawled over Tom's lap. The dog quietly yawned as his master rubbed and twirled his ears. Time with Max relaxed Tom, and that's exactly what he needed at the moment.

"You have to promise me you will never return to that place!" Mrs. Leblanc said. Tom's mother was standing in the middle of his living room, staring down at him. "Are you listening?"

"Yes, Mom," Tom replied.

It had been eleven days since Tom and Julie had returned from Provincetown. They had spent almost all of Sunday trapped on the Cape without power. The innkeeper had been incredibly kind and let them stay a second night at no charge. Power had finally been restored later that evening.

Mother Nature had unleashed quite a storm across New England. Many parts of Massachusetts went three or four days without power. The Outer Cape had been spared the worst of it. At least as far as the storm went. Julie and Tom had rented a car late Monday afternoon and had arrived back in

Providence that evening.

When Tom called his boss to explain what had happened, his boss had insisted Tom take the rest of the week off. Tom was grateful. He needed that time to get new keys for his house and his mom's house. He also had to buy a new phone, tablet, and other accessories. Tom had found the time and energy spent setting up his new gear a great distraction from the whirlwind of emotions he was struggling with.

"Don't 'yes' me, Thomas. Someone tried to kill you and Julie. I still can't believe it. I forbid you to ever go back there!"

Tom began rubbing Max's neck, kneading the skin tightly. Max turned and let out a whimper.

"Sorry," Tom said as he eased his grip on Max. He reached around to Max's stomach and pulled up. Max instinctively rolled over for a belly rub.

His mother sighed as she watched her son focus on his dog, and ignore her.

"Christmas is only ten days away," Mrs. Leblanc said in a softer tone. "I think you need to get some Christmas cheer in here to bring some joy into your home. You haven't put up a single decoration. Not even a tree."

"Mom, I told you I don't want to celebrate this year."

"Well, you leave that to me. I'm going to come back tomorrow and help you decorate."

Tom shook his head. He leaned forward and looked down at Max. Max instinctively reached up and bit his nose. It was a playful, affectionate bite.

"Have you heard anything?" Mrs. Leblanc asked. "From that cop. What was his name? Stevens?"

"Nothing this week," Tom said.

He pushed Max off his lap and stood up. He knew the only way his mom would leave was if he escorted her out. She got the hint and walked to the chair in the corner of the room to retrieve her coat and scarf.

"Well, you let me know when you do, OK?"

"Sure, Mom."

Mrs. Leblanc buttoned up her coat. She wrapped her scarf over the top of her blond/gray hair and firmly tied it beneath her chin.

"And Tom, you need to relax and let the past be the past. You have to let the police do their job, OK? You're no hero."

She stepped forward and reached up to give her son a long hug. Mrs. Leblanc kissed him on the cheek, grabbed her purse, and walked to the front door.

"And Tom, don't worry about presents this year. You are too upset. Let me take care of everything. I bought you several things, but you don't have to worry about getting me a gift. Forget about that candle I asked for. Bye Max!"

***

Tom opened his email on his laptop to see if he had any updates from Officer Stevens. The last one had been five days ago. Tom had emailed him daily since they returned, but most of the responses he had received indicated there was nothing new to report. He checked his Junk folder. Nothing.

A deep growl came from the living room. Max ran to the window and began to bark. The bark quickly changed to a whimper. The front door unbolted and the door opened.

"Max, Max, Max!" Julie called out.

Max ran to greet Julie, jumping on her, his paws landing just a few inches below her chest.

"Watch the Girls, buddy!" Julie warned in a fake stern voice. She leaned down and rubbed noses with Max.

"You missed my mom," Tom said from the kitchen table. "She was here a little while ago."

"Lucky me," Julie replied.

Julie kicked her loose-fitting sneakers off and tossed her coat onto the front chair in the living room. She joined Tom at the kitchen table.

"How was she?"

"The usual. She basically forbade me from ever returning to the Outer Cape. Oh, and I don't have to worry about buying her that candle."

"The candle? Is she serious? That candle was ..."

"Jewels, I never told my mom the full story. About the candle shop. The less she knows, the better. All I told her was some crazy woman broke into the condo and attacked you and said she had taken Chris and Marc."

"And she bought that?"

"Most of it. Luckily the news reports haven't gotten to that level of detail. If I told her I was candle-shopping for her, then this entire thing would become all about her and how this is all her fault. Trust me."

"Wow. Well, I see where you get it from."

"Jewels!"

"Sorry. Any more news from Trevor?"

"Nothing since Monday when he told us about the official missing persons reports that went out. How about you?"

"I called this morning and left him a voicemail but never heard back. I told him about the barn, too. I think we left that out the night we ran to the police station. I can't remember."

"I sent him that as well. We must be driving him crazy."

Tom stood up and walked around the kitchen island. He pulled two martini glasses out of the cupboard, and set about making them drinks.

"I spent the past hour all over social media," Julie sighed. "Still nothing."

"It gets tiring, doesn't it? Posting the pictures and asking people what they might know. Every time I have to explain what happened I just feel like I keep ..."

"Reliving it over and over again?"

Tom nodded as he mixed the drinks.

Julie pulled her phone from her pocket and stared at the screen. She had changed her lock screen image to the group selfie she had taken of her, Marc, Chris, and Tom when they first arrived at the condo.

"Oh, I meant to tell you," Julie said. "I asked my dad where he got that book. I thought it might be something we could tell Trevor. But he didn't remember. He's useless. He said something like, 'Oh, it was a gift shop somewhere on the Cape.' Gee, thanks."

"I searched for that book online, too. I found lots of similar books but nothing that had the same cover. Besides, it's kind of hard to find a book with no author."

"Right? How can you publish something like that?"

"Beats me," Tom sighed. "It just adds to the mystery."

"Did you search for 'FlickerWood Candles,' too?" Julie asked.

"Yes," Tom said. "It was another dead end."

Tom walked back over to the kitchen table carrying the two martini glasses. They were filled to the rim with the light pink cocktail. As he got to the table, he glanced at Julie's phone and saw the picture of them with their friends.

"That's funny," Tom said.

"What?"

He pulled his phone out and held it up to Julie. His lock screen was the same picture. Julie had sent him the photo last week. She smiled as she gazed at the image. Her hazel green eyes filled with tears.

"I still can't believe they're gone," she said softly.

"To hope, then," Tom said as he raised his glass. He felt his eyes begin to well up as he and Julie each took a long sip from their drinks.

"God that's good," Julie said. "I have been craving this all day."

"Ditto on that, Jewels."

Julie's phone rang. It was Officer Stevens.

"Put it on speaker, Jewels."

Julie answered the call and placed the phone to her ear.

"Hi, Trevor. I've got Tom here with me. I'm going to put you on speaker."

Julie placed the phone on the kitchen table.

"Can you guys hear me clearly?" Officer Stevens asked.

"Yes," Tom replied.

"OK, great. Hey, Tom. Glad you are there with Julie. I was going to email you but now I can explain things to both of you at the same time.

"Tom, I appreciate your situation and the concerns you have. I can't respond to all your emails. I hope you understand that."

"I do," Tom replied.

"OK, thanks. I'm trying to be sensitive to everything that has happened."

"So, do you have news about Marc and Chris for us?" Tom asked.

"Not directly. I just got off the phone with Officer Jones out in Truro. It turns out the young Asian couple that owned that store is missing. Their parents came down from Boston to see them shortly after the storm cleared because they hadn't heard from them since before Thanksgiving. They filed an official missing persons report."

"So now there are four missing people?" Tom asked.

"Correct."

"Well, doesn't that sort of help things?" Julie asked. "It makes this a bigger case now, right?"

"Yes and no. Look, guys, I have to be honest with you. If this were four missing children I would think maybe we have some sort of kidnapping or child rapist thing happening. But I've talked with several different detectives about this. We have four adults that have just flat-out disappeared. The store owners have been gone for close to a month now. And your friends disappeared almost two weeks ago. The snow from the storm completely melted away a couple of days after the blizzard ended. The Cape is very narrow. There is only one way out. A big truck like Mr. Sirola had would be hard to miss. Especially with the business signage on it. We've checked all the local hospitals and clinics. There aren't many out here."

Julie glanced over at Tom. Her eyes began to well up.

"So what are you telling us?" Julie asked.

"I'm saying ... I'm saying ... the chances of your friends turning up alive at this point are ... well ... they are remote, at best."

Tom reached across the table and took Julie's hand.

"Listen, guys, I know this is hard to hear. I really thought they were just in a ditch somewhere. But we've been going up and down all the roads out here and there is no sign of that truck at all. With all the time that's passed, I just felt like I needed to be very direct with you. I know this has taken an emotional toll on the two of you."

"So that's it?" Tom asked. "Case closed? What happens now?"

"The case will continue to stay open," Stevens assured him. "This is far from over, OK? But going forward, I need to work with their respective families on this. I just don't want you two obsessing over this every single day. I need to focus my time and energy on working with their family members. This is even more painful for them. I hope you understand."

"It's OK, Trevor," Julie said. She looked over at Tom and nodded.

"And the woman that attacked us?" Tom asked.

"We're working that as well. So far, we've come up dry on finding any Jeep Cherokees like the one you described. At least registered out here. She might have been from out of state. Or unregistered. We are keeping an eye out for someone that meets the description you gave us. But so far nothing."

"You've been great these past weeks," Tom said. "I won't bother you with the daily emails anymore. I'm sorry if that was distracting you. I didn't mean to. But please let us know if anything new comes up."

"I promise to," Stevens said. "You two take care. Try ... try and enjoy the holidays."

The call ended. The screen returned to the lock screen image. Tom let go of Julie's hand and stared at the picture.

"That's it, Jewels," Tom said as tears started to roll down his face. "They're gone ... Marc and Chris are gone. Our friends ... our friends are dead."

Tom turned and looked out of his kitchen window. He reached down and stroked Max's head.

"But we're alive," Julie said. "Because of you. You saved us."

Julie stood up and leaned over and kissed Tom on the cheek. Tears streamed down her face.

"I think we need to try to move forward," Julie continued. It could be weeks if not months before we hear back from Trevor. We can't continue to live in turmoil day after day. We have to start focusing on the positive. We survived. We can mourn the loss of Marc and Chris. We can cherish them. Honor them. We can even hope for a miracle. But we also need to be thankful that we made it out of that nightmare alive. Thanks to you."

"Me? I ... I did sort of save you, didn't I?" Tom said, as if realizing it for the first time.

"I was in total shock in that bed, Tom. All I saw was this torpedo fly across the room and crash into that freak of a woman. She had that knife out, but you never hesitated. You slammed into her like a battering ram."

"It was just as much a blur for me, Jewels. I barely remember doing it."

"My blurry little hero."

Tom smiled and took a long sip of his martini. For the first time in a long time, he felt at ease.

"I know you think I'm crazy," Julie said. "But I really think we got wrapped up in that old urban legend. Those legends are mysteries that never get solved. It's been almost two weeks. No truck. No leads. No ... no bodies. We may never know what happened to them."

"I don't think you're crazy, Jewels. Not anymore. There were just too many coincidences."

Julie smiled, relieved that Tom finally believed her.

"I don't think this is over, Jewels. Not yet. That woman is still out there. Besides, when you read that story, you also said that the bodies always got discovered. Remember?"

"You're right. It did say that, didn't it? I became obsessed with that legend, and read that candle story over a dozen times. I practically have it memorized. How did it end?"

Julie closed her eyes and let her mind take her back to Provincetown. It felt like a lifetime ago. She remembered being curled up on the sectional and opening the book to the chapter on Wellfleet. Her mind cleared and she could see the story page by page, paragraph by paragraph, sentence by sentence, word by word. She recalled the legend's final words.

Julie opened her eyes and looked at Tom and said,

> The killers wanted everyone to know the horror and pain they had inflicted, and that they would eventually strike again.

TWENTY

Wellfleet

It was the Friday before Christmas. The skies were clear, and temperatures were in the mid-40s. The breeze off Wellfleet Harbor was minimal. All of the snow from the blizzard had melted shortly after the storm had passed. The homes and businesses in Wellfleet were covered in joyous Christmas decorations. The shops and restaurants that were open were bustling, as locals enjoyed the mild weather, and tourists scrambled for last-minute gifts.

The old brass bell attached to the entrance of Wellfleet Gifts rang out as the door to the shop swung open. Steve and Leslie Quarry stepped inside and looked around. The recently married couple had spent the day driving in from New York to spend Christmas weekend with Leslie's parents at their vacation home in Wellfleet.

"I'm sure we can find something here," Leslie said.

"I really don't think it's necessary," Steve replied. "Your mom never told you that your sister was going to be in town for Christmas. We don't have to get her a gift. We're running late as it is."

Steve looked down at his watch. It was almost 4 p.m.

"She flew all the way from Kansas as a surprise," Leslie said. "I'm glad my mom let it slip on the phone earlier. I have to get her something! I have to!"

Steve looked around the store. There were no other customers anywhere. The lights were all out. There was a woman behind the counter, hunched over, sweeping the floor.

"Excuse me," Steve called out. "Sorry, but the sign on your door said you were closed. My wife noticed you inside, so we tried the door. It was open. Do you mind if we shop?"

"We won't be long," Leslie added.

The woman looked up and turned to the couple. The right side of her face was disfigured. She had what appeared to be burn marks running from just below her eye all the way down to her chin.

"I was just closing up," Sara said with a smile. "Can I help you find something?"

Leslie walked toward the counter. She tried not to stare at the woman's face. Instead, she rummaged through a clearance bin next to the cash register.

"My sister is visiting from Kansas," Leslie said. "I'd like to get her something ... something ... I don't know, really."

"Something beachy from the Cape?" Sara asked.

"Yes!" Leslie exclaimed. "That would be perfect."

Sara limped as she came around the counter. Her gait was slow and labored. Leslie looked around, trying not to focus on her frail condition. She glanced down at a pile of books on the counter. Leslie grabbed one and read the cover to herself. *Urban Legends of Cape Cod*.

"How about a candle?" Sara asked.

Leslie put the book down. Sara guided them toward the middle of the store and stopped at a small cherry table with inlaid nickel and turquoise legs. The table had a dozen candles stacked on the top of it. They were all glass jars with squared off sides and round tops with hinged lids.

"These are made locally," Sara said. "The wicks are quite unique. They are made from wood. They crackle."

Leslie and Steve each picked up a candle from the table. Steve's candle was brown. He turned it around and looked at the back. There was a simple sticker on it – "FlickerWood

Candles."

"In fact, these were just made last week," Sara said. "You can't get fresher than that."

Leslie looked at the cover of her candle jar. It had a small sticker on top that read "Seabreeze." She flipped the lid open and held the blue candle up to her nose. Steve noticed an old woman emerge from the back room not far from them. She was wearing a long black knit sweater. Her silver hair was pulled back into a bun. She was fiddling with her necklace. Steve found the necklace to be a bit disturbing. He thought it looked like it was made of small bones. The old woman took a few steps forward and smiled.

"Yes, dear," Mother said. "They are scented."

EPILOGUE

If you survived this story, consider yourself one of the lucky ones. Legends never die. They feed on the unsuspecting and relish in their victories. Then they retreat, patiently waiting in silence ... until they can strike again.

Urban Legends of Cape Cod

Author – Unknown

ACKNOWLEDGEMENTS

I have so many people to thank, I truly don't know where to begin. I remember back in a college English class when my teacher gave me positive feedback and encouragement on my writing style. I was studying computer programming at the time. It was the first time I thought to myself, "Maybe I can one day write novels." Just in case the career in IT didn't work out. So, thanks to you, Mr. English Teacher! (Sorry, it was so long ago I don't remember his name.)

As it turns out, the IT career did work out. Over the years, many friends and coworkers who would tell me something along the lines of, "You are such a great storyteller, have you ever thought of writing a book?" And my response to them was always "someday." Their words always helped keep the dream alive. My thanks to all of my friends, family, and coworkers that have pushed me toward my dream.

Publishing my first novel could not have been accomplished without the support of my mom. She has been cheering me on since I started writing this story. Her encouragement, advice, and support were always there when I needed it most.

I also couldn't have produced such a polished document without the help of my team of editors. This version of An Urban Legend is a reissue. The original publication was done in November 2017. Back then I had my sister Lori and my friend Tom play editor. Each had great feedback. After launching my book my friend Terrence introduced me to Lesley Marlow. Her company, Expert Copy, offered to help me refine my story even further.

I turned my story over to Lesley. Her team at Expert Copy did a thorough edit. This wasn't a typical grammar edit. They looked at all aspects of the story. Their feedback was direct and honest. There were a lot of changes needed to elevate my story. It was at this same time that my daytime job went into overdrive. I spent most of 2018 with very little time to devote to reviewing and applying the changes they recommended.

Then in September, a funny thing happened. I got laid off. Suddenly I had no day job. I immediately devoted myself full time to writing. I also attended a fantastic seminar on storytelling. This was also a recommendation from Lesley. I felt it was life-changing. I came home and did a heavy rewrite of the novel. The final product is what you see here. I am looking forward to telling many more stories, and improving my craft with each novel.

ABOUT THE AUTHOR

MJ Howson was born and raised in Providence, Rhode Island. He spent many summers out on Cape Cod as well as the local state beaches in RI. Shortly after turning forty, MJ got a new job that let him work from home. He was no longer tied to his home state for work. Although he had friends and family there, the winters had become too much. He began to work his way south, ultimately ending up in Florida.

MJ was always an entertaining storyteller and often thought to himself, "One day I'll write books." That dream took much longer than expected.

There is a saying: "Life is what happens when you are busy making plans." One day, MJ finally decided to commit the time and dedication to write his first book. A fun fact about MJ is that his plan was to write children's stories. His first book, *Tallow – An Urban Legend*, is anything but a children's story. Shortly before MJ was about to start his first children's book, he had a disturbing dream. He was so rattled by it that he could not get back to sleep. MJ decided to write the details of the dream down. It dawned on him that the nightmare might actually make for a good scary story. He spent the rest of the night working on the outline for what would eventually become his first novel.

MJ adopted the tag line "The Terror is Real" as the focus for the Tallow series of books. Escapist, paranormal, and supernatural stories are always good for a scare. The tales that run the risk of being able to come true, however, are the ones that can really haunt you.

You can connect with MJ via his website. From there you will find links to his different social media accounts.

www.mjhowson.com

www.ingramcontent.com/pod-product-compliance
Lightning Source LLC
Chambersburg PA
CBHW061217170626
46809CB00007B/2514